Swearing und[...] [...] in time to see a skinny fellow with sunken features rushing toward him with a knife.

The blade was clenched in a tight fist and cocked back close to the skinny fellow's ear.

By the time Clint had turned all the way around, the skinny fellow had closed the distance between them and was bringing his blade down in a quick, stabbing motion. Those sunken eyes turned wide in expectation of his kill and his teeth bared as the blade was brought down toward its target.

Clint blinked while the Colt barked once from its spot in his hand. The gun was brought around and aimed like it was an extension of Clint's own arm. It fired with no more than a thought from its wielder and blasted a hole clean through the skinny fellow's body like a rock that had been tossed through wet newspaper.

With the smoke hanging heavy in the air, Clint turned around and brought his gun to bear on the man with the broken nose. The glare on his face was more than enough to freeze the man where he stood. The smoking Colt was enough to get him to drop his own weapon and stumble against the door.

"Start talking," Clint said.

DON'T MISS THESE
ALL-ACTION WESTERN SERIES
FROM THE BERKLEY PUBLISHING GROUP

THE GUNSMITH by J. R. Roberts
Clint Adams was a legend among lawmen, outlaws, and ladies. They called him . . . the Gunsmith.

LONGARM by Tabor Evans
The popular long-running series about Deputy U.S. Marshal Long—his life, his loves, his fight for justice.

SLOCUM by Jake Logan
Today's longest-running action Western. John Slocum rides a deadly trail of hot blood and cold steel.

BUSHWHACKERS by B. J. Lanagan
An action-packed series by the creators of Longarm! The rousing adventures of the most brutal gang of cutthroats ever assembled—Quantrill's Raiders.

DIAMONDBACK by Guy Brewer
Dex Yancey is Diamondback, a Southern gentleman turned con man when his brother cheats him out of the family fortune. Ladies love him. Gamblers hate him. But nobody pulls one over on Dex . . .

WILDGUN by Jack Hanson
The blazing adventures of mountain man Will Barlow—from the creators of Longarm!

TEXAS TRACKER by Tom Calhoun
Meet J. T. Law: the most relentless—and dangerous—manhunter in all Texas. Where sheriffs and posses fail, he's the best man to bring in the most vicious outlaws—for a price.

THE GUNSMITH

282

THE LAST RIDE

J. R. ROBERTS

JOVE BOOKS, NEW YORK

THE BERKLEY PUBLISHING GROUP
Published by the Penguin Group
Penguin Group (USA) Inc.
375 Hudson Street, New York, New York 10014, USA
Penguin Group (Canada), 10 Alcorn Avenue, Toronto, Ontario M4V 3B2, Canada
(a division of Pearson Penguin Canada Inc.)
Penguin Books Ltd., 80 Strand, London WC2R 0RL, England
Penguin Group Ireland, 25 St. Stephen's Green, Dublin 2, Ireland (a division of Penguin Books Ltd.)
Penguin Group (Australia), 250 Camberwell Road, Camberwell, Victoria 3124, Australia
(a division of Pearson Australia Group Pty. Ltd.)
Penguin Books India Pvt. Ltd., 11 Community Centre, Panchsheel Park, New Delhi—110 017, India
Penguin Group (NZ), Cnr. Airborne and Rosedale Roads, Albany, Auckland 1310, New Zealand
(a division of Pearson New Zealand Ltd.)
Penguin Books (South Africa) (Pty.) Ltd., 24 Sturdee Avenue, Rosebank, Johannesburg 2196,
South Africa

Penguin Books Ltd., Registered Offices: 80 Strand, London WC2R 0RL, England

This is a work of fiction. Names, characters, places, and incidents either are the product of the author's imagination or are used fictitiously, and any resemblance to actual persons, living or dead, business establishments, events, or locales is entirely coincidental.

THE LAST RIDE

A Jove Book / published by arrangement with the author

PRINTING HISTORY
Jove edition / June 2005

Copyright © 2005 by Robert J. Randisi.

ISBN: 0-515-13957-2

JOVE®
Jove Books are published by The Berkley Publishing Group,
a division of Penguin Group (USA) Inc.,
375 Hudson Street, New York, New York 10014.
JOVE is a registered trademark of Penguin Group (USA) Inc.
The "J" design is a trademark belonging to Penguin Group (USA) Inc.

PRINTED IN THE UNITED STATES OF AMERICA

10 9 8 7 6 5 4 3 2 1

ONE

West Texas may have been no-man's-land to some, but for Clint Adams, it was the closest thing he had to a home. That fact suited him just fine since he normally spent most of his time charging into places that most men knew better than to go anywhere near.

Between the people trying to get him to work for their own ends or the ones who just plain wanted to see him dead, Clint got more than his share of excitement without even having to look for it. After a heaping portion of that, a little peace and quiet was always a good thing.

He could feel the moment he'd crossed into Texas. Like most experienced riders, he knew the landmarks well enough, but those weren't what tipped him off. Crossing over into Texas was like stepping from one yard into another. The ground felt as though it was a bit more suited to his steps and the air started to smell just a little bit sweeter.

Eclipse might have felt the change as well, since the Darley Arabian stallion's pace became a bit more relaxed. The horse hadn't been riding full out for some time, but now that he was back on a familiar trail, he finally seemed to relax.

Leaning forward, Clint reached out and patted the horse's neck. "It won't be long now, boy," he said. "Both of us will sleep comfortably tonight. And the food will be better as well. Then again, anything would beat another night of free grazing."

Whether he understood anything that Clint was saying or whether he was just responding to the familiar touch upon his mane, Eclipse nodded slowly and kept walking steadily onward.

The Darley Arabian hadn't been feeling right for a while. Some time ago, he'd gotten cut by the blade of some wild-eyed killer looking to prevent Clint from following him. Although the wound had been treated properly at the time, Eclipse never really got a chance to rest up before he was required to take off again like a bolt of lightning.

Even then, Clint hadn't noticed anything wrong with the stallion until just recently. Normally, Eclipse loved to run more than anything else in the world. Some horses worked just fine pulling a plough. Others worked best in a team and others were made to charge into combat.

Eclipse had been around more than enough gunfire that he didn't so much as flinch when shots whipped past his head. But, more than anything else, the Darley Arabian loved to run. Clint had covered more miles in less time than he'd ever thought possible on the back of that horse. That was how he was able to pick up on the first sign that Eclipse might be hurting.

He'd spotted it the way he might pick up on the dark mood of a friend. Eclipse's head was hanging lower than usual and he just didn't respond to the flick of the reins the way he used to. Sure, the stallion could still run like the wind, but the joy just wasn't there.

Putting those pieces together, Clint immediately thought back to Duke. The big, black gelding he'd ridden before Eclipse had simply gotten too old to put up with the strain of the trail and had to be put out to pasture. Although things could have been a whole lot worse, Clint still missed the old boy every now and then.

More than anything else, however, he didn't want to part ways with Eclipse just yet. Although he knew the Darley Arabian still had plenty of miles left to ride, Clint wasn't going to take any chances where a friend was concerned.

Settling back into the saddle, Clint draped the reins over one knee and let the Darley Arabian plod along the trail at his own pace. "You'll get yourself a nice stable and some greens," he said. "You'll also get to rest those legs of yours for a while before you need to pull off any more miracle rides."

With West Texas being a harsh expanse of flat terrain, the town Clint was headed for was almost in sight. It would be a while before they reached it, but he knew they could make it not too much after sundown.

When they finally did ride down the familiar street into Labyrinth, Clint could feel Eclipse's steps becoming slower and more deliberate. He didn't really think the horse understood much of what was spoken to him, but he sure seemed to know when he was home.

The stallion was leaning into turns before Clint even thought about tugging the reins. Every now and then, Clint would have sworn that Eclipse stepped around holes in the road that had been there the last time they were in town.

Reflexively, Eclipse started to walk in the direction of what would normally be Clint's first stop when he got into Labyrinth. Rick's Place was a saloon owned by Clint's good friend Rick Hartman. But he wasn't headed there just yet, and Clint indicated that much with a subtle nudge from his heel.

"Not just yet, boy. Let's get you situated first."

Clint could have steered Eclipse to the stables with his eyes shut. That was one of the finest things about being in such a welcoming, familiar place. Apart from a few exceptions here and there, everything important was right where he'd left it the last time he was in town.

"There you go, boy," Clint said after putting Eclipse up in

a stall for the night. "I'll check in on you in the morning."

The liveryman shook his head when Clint offered him a down payment for renting the stall. "That won't be necessary, Mister Adams. We can settle up before you leave."

"Are you sure? I can at least pay for the food."

"Nah. Looking after ol' Eclipse here is payment enough."

Clint nodded and tipped his hat before turning to head out the door. Before he could leave, he was stopped by the liveryman's voice.

"Welcome back, Mister Adams."

"It's good to be here." At that moment, he couldn't have been more sincere.

TWO

Rick's Place might not have been Clint's first stop this time around, but it was an awfully close second. With his saddlebags still slung over his shoulder, Clint headed down the street and made a line straight for the familiar saloon.

It was well past dark, but that didn't mean much to the men who crowded around the bar and at the various gaming tables inside the place. Clint couldn't help but smile when he stepped through the front door and pulled in a lungful of the smoky air.

"Well I'll be damned," a familiar voice boomed. "Just when I thought I got rid of the bad element, it comes stumbling through my door."

Rick Hartman stood behind the bar with both hands pressed against the polished top. His posture made it seem as though he was about to jump over the bar at any second and charge the front door. A few of the men with drinks became a bit tense at the display. The regulars, on the other hand, knew better.

"You want me out?" Clint asked as he took one more step inside and planted both feet firmly in place. "You've got to come out from around that bar and toss me out yourself."

"Yeah?" Rick reached beneath the bar and found something which he brought up. "Maybe I don't have to move from this spot." With that, he lifted the bottle he'd been holding and threw it through the air toward Clint.

Clint's hand snatched the bottle from the air without him really having to think about it. Still holding the bottle in front of him, he turned it so he could get a look at the label. "What's this?" he asked.

"My own brew," Hartman beamed. "Have a swig for yourself."

The bottle was smaller than any other liquor bottle and filled with a foaming, dark liquid. After pulling out the cork, Clint sniffed the stuff for himself and found it to be a dark, rich beer. He took a sip and winced dramatically.

"Jesus, Rick. Are you trying to kill me with this stuff?"

The bluster that had been on Rick's face before faded instantly and his arms dropped down to his sides. "What? You don't like it?"

Clint was already at the bar so he could set the bottle down before dropping his saddlebags onto the floor beside him. "That depends on if you want me to drink it or polish the floor with it."

Although the initial tension from some of the others in the bar had vanished, it soon came back again when Clint said that about the beer.

Hartman leaned forward so one elbow was braced against the bar. Glaring across at Clint, he fixed his eyes upon him and said, "To hell with you, Adams."

Clint did his best to keep a stern look on his face, but he only managed to hold it for another second or two before breaking into a wide smile. "How the hell have you been, Rick?" he asked while reaching out to shake the other man's hand.

"Just fine until you walked in. You better hope that ugly face of yours don't scare away the customers."

Lifting the bottle, Clint tipped it back so he could take a long sip. The brew was strong and did a damn fine job of washing away the dust that had collected in his throat after such a long ride. It even left a taste behind that made him nod in appreciation.

"What do you think?" Hartman asked. "I came up with that brew myself. Got so many compliments on it, I've been kicking around the notion of selling it."

"I don't know much about selling beer, but I'd say you could do a whole lot worse."

"Coming from you, that's a hell of a compliment."

That seemed to be enough to put everyone at ease so the customers in the saloon could get back to whatever they'd been doing before Clint had arrived. A few of the newer faces whispered amongst themselves regarding who Clint was and what he was doing there. A few of the locals gave Clint a quick wave before turning back to their conversations. A few more started working their way over to Clint's spot without making too big of a show of it.

"So what brings you back to Labyrinth?" Hartman asked.

"Eclipse is due for a rest and this seemed like the best place for it."

Hartman straightened up again. His face became deadly serious and the tone in his voice dropped to an almost threatening level. "You didn't hurt that horse, did you?"

"No, nothing like that. He could just use some time to sit still, is all."

"Well, not that it ain't good to see you, but why come here just for that? Aren't there plenty of other liveries out there that were suited for something like that?"

"Let's just say that I'd rather not leave him with someone I don't know."

That tone returned to Hartman's voice, only this time it wasn't aimed directly at Clint. "I don't like the sound of that. You have a scrape with horse thieves?"

"Not exactly." Clint paused so he could take another sip of Hartman's beer. As the brew washed down his throat, he thought back to the blade that had been dragged across Eclipse's ankle. "Just a close call with some asshole who was too yellow to come at me with his knife."

"So he cut on a horse?" Rick asked disbelievingly. "That son of a bitch. I hope it's nothing too bad."

"Nah. I got to him before he could do any real damage. Still, that doesn't mean that Eclipse doesn't deserve some rest. I'd just feel better knowing there's someone around I can trust to keep an eye on him."

Before he said another word, Hartman leveled his gaze at Clint and kept it there. As the seconds ticked by, Clint started to squirm more and more in front of him. Finally, Rick broke the silence.

"You could keep watch on him just fine yourself, Clint. What's the catch?"

"No catch." Clint paused to take another sip of beer. When he looked back across the bar, Hartman was still staring straight back at him. "Actually, I was wondering if you might do me a favor."

"There it is. Just what I was waiting for. Let's hear it."

"Do I really need to spell it out?"

"No," Hartman said, easing off so he could wipe off the bar. "I'd be happy to look in on Eclipse for you. And if anyone so much as breathes on him funny, I'll make him walk funny for the rest of his life."

"Thanks. I appreciate it."

"Where you off to this time that you can't stick around here for a bit?"

"Tombstone. A friend of mine in the US Marshals asked me to help in transporting some prisoners to a prison out in the middle of nowhere."

Hartman whistled under his breath. "I don't know which makes me more uncomfortable: that these prisoners need a federal escort to be dumped into some hole in the sand or that those Marshals want you to go along for the ride. Either way, these must be some bad men."

"That's what I like about you," Clint said, lifting his bottle in a sarcastic salute. "You're always looking at the bright side of things."

Smirking and lifting the glass he'd just been polishing, Hartman said, "Well, if it's good news you're after, then all you need to do is turn around."

Clint did just that and was just in time to brace himself as someone rushed him with enough force to knock him roughly against the bar.

THREE

Clint barely had enough time to react before he was over-powered by the person who was charging straight for him. If he hadn't been so tired and hadn't just downed some damn potent beer, he would have been able to hear the other person before they'd gotten half as close. But, even with all his wits about him, Clint wouldn't have changed a single thing.

In fact, getting stampeded by someone as pretty as Emily Singer was a pleasure all its own.

"Clint Adams," the tall woman with flowing brown hair said as she pushed herself against him. "When were you going to get around to telling me you would be in town?"

"Just as soon as I was done with this beer." After saying that, Clint tipped the bottle back and drained the rest of the brew. He tossed it over his shoulder and Rick was just barely able to catch it before it shattered against the top of the bar.

"There," Clint said, leaning back while thoroughly enjoying the weight of Emily against him. "Now I'm done. Good thing you're here. I was just about to come and tell you I was in town."

Emily was able to look Clint in the eyes without having

to look up very much at all. The tall heels on her boots accounted for some of that, but the rest was all her own height. She stood in front of Clint, wrapped in a dress that was black with threads of different colors sewn throughout the material. Red lace fringe hung along the hem and sleeves, as well as along the neckline.

Speaking of which, that neckline plunged down to an almost dangerous level to display a generous amount of cleavage. Her body was solid and with more than enough curves to keep any man's hands busy for a good, long time. Emily's hair flowed all around her face in large, chestnut brown waves. Hazel eyes glinted hungrily at Clint as she gently licked her soft, pink lips.

"You always were a smart-ass," she said while grabbing hold of Clint's arms and pulling him closer.

"And you always knew how to make an entrance. Looks like neither one of us has lost our touch."

"Nope," she said, reaching down to feel quickly between his legs, "we sure haven't."

"Don't mean to be rude," Rick said. "But I don't run that type of place. You want a room, there's always one for ya. But this ain't exactly the floor show I'm after."

Clint was allowed to come up for air for about a second and a half before he felt Emily take hold of his hand.

"Come on with me," she said, dragging him toward the door. "I've got just the right kind of welcome in mind for you."

Even before he could get hold of his saddlebags, Clint was hauled out the front door.

Rick was already walking around the bar to retrieve the bags. "Don't worry, Clint," he said while lifting the bags up and tossing them behind the bar. "I'll watch these for ya."

Emily lived only a few minute's walk from Rick's Place. She only had to drag Clint a couple of yards before he was the one leading the way. Soon, they were inside again and making their way into her bedroom. The only thing that made the process difficult was the fact that neither one of them could keep their hands off each other.

Stepping back just to put some space between them, Emily lit a few candles that were scattered about her bedroom. Soon, the room was illuminated by a soft, warm glow.

"If I knew you were coming to town," she whispered, "I would have been able to get ready for you."

"Don't you like surprises?"

Keeping her eyes locked upon him, she eased forward while reaching out to pull open his shirt. "There are some things that I like a whole lot better."

With that, she slipped her hands under Clint's shirt and massaged the muscles of his chest. His hands were busy as well, easing up and down the generous curves of her hips and breasts. Emily's breathing started to match the pace of his touch.

She breathed in slowly as his hands wandered up and settled upon her breasts. The material of her dress clung tightly to her body, but her erect nipples were still able to be felt through it.

She let her breath out again as his hands moved slowly down her sides once more, settling upon her hips and easing around to cup her backside.

Even through the layers of skirts she wore, Clint could feel the soft skin of her rounded buttocks. The lacy undergarments shifted beneath the skirts, sliding against her skin as Clint's strong hands explored her inch by inch.

"Good lord," Emily said as she reached down to pull open Clint's jeans. "I swear that I dream about the way you touch me."

Clint eased her skirts up bit by bit until he was able to slip his hand up underneath them. "You know what I dream about?" he asked.

Before she could answer, Emily's breath was taken away

from her. Clint had found his way to her lace panties and then slid the tips of his fingers beneath them.

The skin of her inner thighs was softer than the silk Emily wore. As he felt his way up higher, the texture only got smoother until Clint made it to the soft patch of downy hair. Clint held on to her tightly, knowing that she would start to sway once he began gently massaging her moistening lips.

"Damn," she breathed as a shudder worked its way through her body. "It's good to have you back."

FOUR

The prison located just outside of Houston wasn't much more than a brick with a few barred windows. Even without the bars, those windows weren't much bigger than a brick or two themselves. A child might have been able to reach out through the hole and get a feel of fresh air on his hand, but not much more than that.

As for the men locked up in that prison, they hadn't felt fresh air for months. For some of them, it had been years.

For David Trask and John Redwater, it had been just over a decade.

Redwater had been the first one to land in the prison, but that had only been after a chase that had lasted for six weeks and taken three posses through some of the most hellish terrain the country could offer. Along the way, Redwater had slaughtered nine men and that didn't even take into account the dozen or so armed robberies that had put the price on his head to begin with.

The only thing that had saved Redwater's life was the fact that he hadn't left enough of the bodies to make it clear exactly how they'd died. After sifting through the gory mess, lawmen couldn't say for certain whether it had been Redwater who'd done the killing or if it had been some wild animal.

Some of the remains that were found couldn't even be identified as human.

The fact of the matter was that nobody had actually seen him kill anybody.

Without those things working in his favor, he would have been swinging from the end of a rope a long time ago. Of course, that would have required a whole lot of people without regard for their own lives to get close enough to try and cinch that noose around his neck.

Redwater was a mix of Cherokee and Sioux. According to the stories floating through both nations, Redwater was some kind of devil or vicious trickster. He arrived in shadow, lured folks off on their own and disappeared. The only thing he ever left behind was the rivers of blood which eventually became his namesake.

Even the big Indian himself didn't call himself by his proper name after that.

Leaning against the wall with both hands pressed flat against the stony surface, John Redwater stared out through the rectangular hole that was his only view to the outside world. The windows were placed at slightly above average eye level, but Redwater still had to slouch to get a good look through it.

His arms were thick with muscle and his fingers clawed against the wall as though he was about to try and pull it down. Judging by the massive, trunklike arms and thick barrel chest, one might have thought that he had a good shot of doing just that. If not, the burning, intense fire in his eyes might just melt a hole big enough for him to walk through.

Sitting in a corner of another cell was Dave Trask.

Unlike Redwater, Trask didn't bother looking through the window in his cell. Even when the sun shone through it for about a minute or two each day, Trask avoided the rays as if they would do physical damage to him.

Trask was a wiry man of average height with a head full of thick black hair. The stubble on his face was so dense that it looked more like an oil slick that had seeped onto his skin and wasn't about to budge. Sitting with his shoulders propped against the wall, Trask might have been mistaken for a dead man due to the fact that he rarely moved.

Like Redwater, Trask was a killer. The main difference was that he wasn't quite as messy as the Indian. The men he killed simply disappeared and were never seen again. They just seemed to have taken a wrong turn and disappeared forever.

A few bodies were found, but the only thing that could be said about them was that they were dead. No witnesses remained to say who'd killed them. At least, no witnesses remained who were stupid enough to say a word against Dave Trask.

Without enough evidence to convince a judge or a lynch mob brave enough to step in, David Trask and John Redwater were handled in the next best way. They were sent somewhere far away from civilized folks so they could rot.

The bodies stopped falling.

The blood stopped flowing.

The threat was dealt with and two stone cold killers were never to be heard from again.

It wouldn't be long, however, before all of that was changed in a big way.

FIVE

Clint woke up the next morning in one of the best ways humanly possible.

At first, he thought he was having a dream. His loins were on fire in a way that gave him all of the heat and none of the pain. It was a kind of fire that traveled all throughout his flesh until he thought he was about to burst from the buildup of so much intense pleasure.

Just when he was about to lay back and savor the dream for all it was worth, he realized that he wasn't dreaming at all. Instead, he was still in Emily's bed wearing nothing but the wide smile on his face. As for Emily, she was moving beneath the covers, her hands slowly kneading the muscles of his chest and stomach while her head bobbed up and down between his legs.

Without opening his eyes, Clint reached down under the sheet that was covering him until he found the soft, rumpled mess of Emily's hair. He threaded his fingers through the silky tangle while she continued to move up and down over his growing erection. Her lips wrapped around his cock tightly at the base so she could suck as she moved her head up until she reached the tip. There, she let her tongue dance around the sensitive end of his penis before she opened her lips a bit and slid them all the way down his length once more.

Clint could feel her smile without having to open his eyes in the least. When he did take a look for himself, Emily was slowly coming up again while looking straight up at his face.

She let him slip from her mouth, but kept hold of him with one hand. "I thought it was time to get you up," she said.

Clint smiled and leaned back into the pillow. "You did a damn fine job of that."

Stroking him in long, smooth motions, she slid up over him until she was forced to let go of his solid erection. The instant her hand broke contact, however, she straddled him just enough for the wet lips of her pussy to slide against his rigid column of flesh.

"Now that you're up," Emily purred. "I say we take full advantage of it."

Clint responded to that by reaching out with both hands and taking hold of Emily. One hand slid up along one side while the other got a firm grasp of her hip. From there, he shifted quickly and flipped both of them onto their sides.

Emily squirmed against him, grinding her hips in the perfect way to coax him to an even more powerful erection. As she felt Clint growing harder between her legs, Emily smiled mischievously.

"You feel pretty awake to me," she said.

"I sure am."

When Clint reached around to take hold of her, Emily moved back instead. Although she allowed him to slip inside of her, she only took an inch or so of his cock into her before she placed a hand on him and pushed him back.

Before Clint could say anything, he felt her wriggle around until she'd positioned herself on her opposite side with her back pressed against him. Emily's plump, firm backside moved against his rigid penis and Clint let his eyes wander slowly along the perfect curve of her spine.

Leaning back so her head was resting against Clint's shoulder, Emily lifted one leg up and hooked it over him. All she had to do then was shift her hips and his cock was once again sliding along the wet lips between her thighs.

Clint reached around and brushed his fingers against the swollen nub of her clitoris. When she began trembling with pleasure, he felt her hand guiding his cock between her legs until it began to enter her pussy from behind.

Their bodies were spooned together, with Emily's back arched just enough for him to be able to pump into her freely. One leg was sliding against his while her other leg was draped completely over him.

From where he was, Clint was able to kiss and nibble Emily's neck while reaching around to cup her firm, rounded breasts. The angle from which he was entering her allowed him to hit the spot inside of Emily's body that sent her almost immediately into an orgasm.

As her body shook and trembled with the climax, she reached behind her to slide her fingers through Clint's hair while her hips pumped furiously along his cock.

Once Emily's body started to go limp from exhaustion, Clint rolled her onto her back and settled on top of her. She opened her legs for him immediately and closed her eyes while letting out a sigh as he slipped his entire length inside of her.

Now, it seemed as though Emily was the one who thought she was dreaming. As Clint pumped in and out of her, she closed her eyes and writhed against the pillows. Whispers came from her mouth, but weren't loud enough to be understood. Clint didn't have any trouble whatsoever in understanding the moans that started to grow from the back of her throat.

The pleasure was starting to come to a boil inside of

him now and Clint let himself fully savor every second of it. While rising up over her, he moved his hands along the smooth skin of her belly and then up to the mounds of her breasts and finally to the dark, erect nipples.

Once both of his hands came to a rest upon her generous breasts, Clint gave in to his own desires and started pounding into her with growing force.

Emily's legs curled against the bed as she took him inside of her.

Clint eased in and out with perfect fluidity since she was wet and spread open just for him. After a few more powerful thrusts, he exploded inside of her and they both let out a groan that echoed throughout her entire house.

After a few seconds, Emily's eyes slowly came open and a warm smile drifted onto her face.

"As much as I'd like to do that again," she said, "I just can't. Some of us need to work for a living."

Clint winced and rolled onto the bed beside her. "That was just cruel."

"I just wanted to see the look on your face when I'm the one that needs to ride off somewhere else. And you know what? It was worth it."

Clint didn't let her get off that easily. Reaching out to grab hold of her, he wrestled her to the mattress and started placing gentle kisses along the front of her body.

She squirmed, giggled and pretended to resist for all of three seconds.

SIX

The prison itself didn't have a name.

It was one of those places that was built to be something almost as good as death and there were plenty of them scattered throughout the country. The guards could do whatever they wanted just so long as they didn't draw too much attention to themselves.

Of course, with the type of scum populating those places, the guards were just fine to keep their distance and throw the prisoners' food at them through the bars of their cages. One of the few guards who weren't afraid of the animals in their charge was named Smitty Green.

Smitty was a big fellow with a gut that tested the limits of his starched white shirt and uniform jacket. He had a stout build beneath all that blubber and most of that came from the constant work of swinging his club or slamming his boots into exposed rib cages.

Walking down the aisle between the two rows of cells, Smitty made sure to knock his club against every bar and whistle piercingly enough to wake the dead. When he got in the aisle between Trask's and Redwater's cells, he stopped and rocked idly on his heels.

"Looks like you two get to leave this place soon,"

21

Smitty said. "Of course, I wouldn't be too happy about that if I was you."

He waited for a response from the prisoners, but got nothing. Emboldened by that, Smitty kept right on talking in his mocking, almost singsong tone of voice.

"You boys have been very naughty in here. Just because you're locked up don't mean you get to do whatever the fuck you want." Shifting his eyes to Redwater, he squared off and stared right at the back of the Indian's head.

"And you, red man. You think you can get away with killing poor ol' Jimmy McBarry? Sure, he was a pain in the ass, but that don't mean you get to twist his head around." Stepping up until he was almost kissing the bars, Smitty added, "But your real mistake was in punching a guard when they came to clean up the body. We don't put up with that shit around here, red man. You should'a learned that by now."

Again, Smitty waited to see what Redwater would say to that. He was certain he would get the Indian to lash out or even say anything. He was so certain, in fact, that he had the keys in his hand to unlock the cell door so he could go in there and cave in the side of Redwater's skull.

"And you," Smitty said, turning around so he could glare at David Trask. "You should've known better than to beat ol' Halliwell to a pulp right in front of me. I mean, what the hell did you think you were gonna accomplish? Now you're both headed off to that new prison up in Arizona where you'll be all by your lonesome.

"A few weeks in that place and you'll be praying for death. A few weeks more, and you'll do yerselves in. After all, what do you think happened to the last prisoners that were in there? And why do you think it's empty now?"

Once again, Smitty waited to see what kind of response he would get from the prisoners.

Redwater stood so completely still that it wasn't obvious that he was even still breathing.

Trask shifted his eyes toward the guard and started to say something, but stopped himself before making a sound.

That reaction from Trask, however, was more than enough to suit the guard's purpose.

"Oh, you didn't like that, did ya?" Smitty asked as he turned so that he was looking straight into Trask's cell. "Well, it don't matter much what you like or don't like. From what I hear, you two will be getting to stand in front of a new judge and this one won't be so forgiving as the last one.

"And as for the jury? You can just forget about them too. This country's paid to keep you alive for too damn long. So enjoy those free meals while they last, because it won't be much longer before you won't be eating nothing but the dirt that drops in through the cracks of yer coffin lid."

Proud of himself, Smitty leaned forward and grinned into the cell. What little sunlight that could make it into the block-like building was reflected against the dust that had been kicked up by Smitty's steps. That dust swirled about the guard's face and was sucked in through his nose as he stood waiting to see what Trask would do next.

"Come on, boy," Smitty taunted. "I know there's something you want to say to me. Just say whatever's on yer mind because soon we won't be seeing each other anymore."

Trask gritted his teeth. His eyes cut through the shadows and his face twitched sporadically.

The couple of other prisoners inside the other cells kept quiet as well. That was mostly so they didn't draw Smitty's attention, since that usually was accompanied by the crack of his club against their heads.

After waiting a few more seconds, Smitty relaxed a bit and shook his head. "You got nothing to say, huh? Well that's about what I expected. Between that piece of shit red man and you, I've learned that the only thing you're good for is killing women or them that can't fend for themselves."

In his cell, Trask leaned back against his wall and let his fists relax as a smile worked its way onto his face.

"Yeah, you go ahead and smile, you piece of shit," Smitty said. "You just know that I'm right."

The guard heard a slight rustle behind him, but not enough to warrant his immediate attention. When he heard something brush against rusty iron bars, it was too late for him to do a damn thing about it.

Redwater's arm snaked through the bars and his fingers clamped hard around Smitty's windpipe. The Indian pinched the guard's throat shut so no breath or even a single peep could escape as Smitty was pulled back against Redwater's cell.

"You don't talk about me," Redwater hissed into Smitty's ear. "Not any more."

As he snaked his massive arm between the bars to finish Smitty off, Redwater felt in the guard's pockets with his other hand. Smitty flopped against the bars and his eyes started bugging out of his head. Soon, he felt as though he was being lifted off the ground.

Smitty never got a look at Redwater. All he could see was Trask inching closer and closer to his own bars to watch with a wide, gleeful smile.

SEVEN

Clint took his time walking down the streets on his way back to Rick's Place. It did him good to follow the familiar path and nod to a few familiar faces. Although he wasn't in Labyrinth as much as he might have liked, Clint was friendly enough with the locals to be always considered one of them. And they, in turn, were some of the few people in the country who remembered him as Clint Adams and not just The Gunsmith.

The difference was subtle, but very noticeable to Clint. When he stopped to occasionally shoot the breeze with someone, the conversation never once turned to any gunfight or supposed sharpshooting feat. Talk centered mostly on boring things like the weather or whose kids were winning spelling bees.

Boring to some, but a breath of clean, fresh air to Clint.

By the time he actually stepped into Rick's Place, Clint was wearing a smile that went from one ear to another.

"Well, well," Rick said from where he was cleaning off a table across the room. "Looks like someone had a real good night."

Clint started to say that he wasn't smiling about anything like that, but he couldn't exactly deny Rick's claim.

25

Instead, he shrugged and took a seat at the table Rick was cleaning. "And a good day to go right along with it," Clint said.

"Well, you've earned a few of those. Have you had any coffee yet? I just brewed up a fresh pot."

"Sounds good."

"All right, then. Come on along with me and speak your mind. You look like you got something to say."

"Remind me to never play poker with you, Rick. You can read me like a book."

"Now why would I want to remind you of something as foolish as that?" Rick asked, doing his best to sound offended. "Especially when I need some money to fix up my roof."

Clint followed Rick to the end of the bar farthest from the door and closest to the back wall. Apparently, Rick knew enough about the surprises that sometimes cropped up in Clint's life to know that it was always best to keep one eye on the door and his back to the wall.

"What's on yer mind?" Rick asked as he poured out a cup of thick, dark coffee from a steaming pot and set it onto the bar.

"Nothing too pressing," Clint said. "Just relaxing for a bit before taking on this job."

"That job you were talking about doesn't sound like anything too bad. Of course, it's not like I could do it so much better."

Clint took hold of the dented tin cup that Rick had put down in front of him. Already, the metal was warm to the touch and felt just as familiar as the walk through the front door. The coffee inside was a typical saloon brew. Made more to open a drunk's eyes rather than complement breakfast, the thick, dark concoction was potent as hell.

Even before Clint got any of the coffee into his mouth, the smell of it was strong enough to make him sit up and take notice. Having the coffee trickle down his throat had the same effect as suddenly dunking his head into a bucket of cold water.

"If it was that easy," Clint said while bracing one foot against the rail running the length of the bar, "the Marshals wouldn't have needed anyone's help."

"Yeah, I kinda figured that was the case. Folks usually don't call on you unless they think there's a good chance for some trouble."

"Well, it shouldn't be anything too bad. They just wanted to have someone they could trust who wasn't a Marshal."

"You mean an unfamiliar face?"

"I guess you could say that."

Rick chuckled and started wiping off a spot on the bar.

"What's so funny?" Clint asked.

"The thought of you being an unfamiliar face. You're better known than the president around here."

"I meant as a face that's not a US Marshal, smart-ass. By the way, this coffee stinks."

Rather than shoot back with another jibe, Rick accepted that last one and moved on. "So, go on with what you were saying."

"Just that there might be some messages coming through here for me. The job involves transferring a couple of prisoners from one place to another and it's a pretty long haul."

"Why not just let them rot wherever they are?"

"Because they're stirring up so much shit that they're better off somewhere else. Besides, the real concern is that too many people know where these prisoners are being held. It's gotten to the point that they're waiting for a jail-break any day now."

Rick nodded and gave a low whistle. "Sounds like they got their hands full."

"Yeah. The fact that the prisoners are being moved has already been printed in a few newspapers, but the Marshals are keeping the route they're taking a secret. That's why I couldn't say anything when this place was full of people yesterday."

"So why tell me?" Rick asked.

"Because I'm not a US Marshal and if I want you to help me out a little it's only fair you have a notion of what's going on."

"I appreciate that, Clint. But if you're violating any confidences, then you don't have to—"

"I know I don't have to," Clint interrupted. "But there's no reason for me not to trust you."

Rick nodded again. This time, it was a gesture of admiration as well as loyalty. There wasn't many men who either of them could trust implicitly. But the two men talking at the far end of the bar trusted each other with their lives.

"I need to catch a stage out of here this afternoon," Clint said. "From there, I'll be meeting up with a train bound for Tombstone and then move onto another stage. The thing is that the route might be changed at a moment's notice and the Marshals want to be able to get a message to me if that happens. They don't want to tip their hand as to who their unfamiliar face is so they needed someone else to contact."

Rick nodded. "And that's where I come in."

"You got it."

"So I just need to check in at the telegraph office from time to time?"

"Actually, about three times a day. If there is a message waiting for me, I'll need to know right away. I'll be checking in as often as I can and might need you to be ready to make a run down the street to answer me real quickly."

Rolling his eyes dramatically, Rick tossed the rag he'd been using to the floor and said, "You better be paying me extra for that kind of crap."

"How about I forgive the money you still owe me from when you tried for that inside straight?"

"How about you buy me a steak when you get back?"

Clint extended a hand and said, "You always did drive a hard bargain. Think I could impose on you a bit further?"

"No need to ask. I'll check in on Eclipse for you to make sure he's resting up properly."

"You're a hell of a friend, Rick. I really appreciate all of this."

"Hey, after all the times you've put your neck on the line for me, I'd say this isn't too much trouble at all."

Clint stayed at the saloon for a little while longer so he could finish off his coffee. Although the brew was strong enough to strip the varnish off of wood, the conversation more than made up for it.

EIGHT

Before leaving town, Clint checked in on Eclipse. Just by laying down for a while and being tended to, the Darley Arabian was looking much better. There was still a tiredness in his eyes that remained even as he struggled to get up when Clint walked into the stables.

"Easy, boy," Clint said as he stepped up to Eclipse's stall and urged the stallion back down onto his bed of straw. "No need to get up on my account."

"Mr. Adams?"

The voice was nasal and somewhat scratchy. The man who'd spoken was about Clint's height, but gave away at least seventy pounds to the other man. Even so, he stepped forward with confidence and put himself between Clint and Eclipse's stall.

"I'm Clint Adams."

The skinny man relaxed a bit and stepped aside again. "I'm Marvin Hennessey, the vet looking after Eclipse here."

Clint shook the hand that was offered and was more than a little surprised at the doctor's strong grip.

"Sorry about the bad first impression," Hennessey said,

"but I've learned to be careful when treating such fine animals as this. You know, horse thieves and such."

"Has that been a problem around here lately?"

"Not as such, but it did happen once to me. That one time was enough." Glancing around at the other stalls, Hennessey lowered his voice even though none of the other horses seemed to care whether he was even there or not. "I'm especially careful in this case. I haven't seen such a fine Darley Arabian for some time."

"How's he doing?"

"Oh, not too bad. That wound on his leg could use some more time to heal up properly and he could do with some rest. Other than that, he's in excellent condition."

"Good. He just didn't seem like himself."

"Well, I wouldn't worry. Horses are just like people. They work as hard as they can, but they can use a vacation every now and then."

"Will a week or two be enough?"

Hennessey squinted and glanced in at the dressing that was loosely wrapped around the scar on Eclipse's leg. "If that wound was any worse, I'd say no. But whoever patched it up in the first place did a good enough job. A week should be fine."

Clint nodded and stepped up to the stall. Despite the word from his doctor, Eclipse got up on his own and walked up to nuzzle Clint's hand. The familiar spark was already rekindling in Eclipse's eyes.

"Yeah," Clint said to the stallion. "Sometimes even the best of us needs a little time off."

Unfortunately, this wasn't Clint's time to indulge himself in this way.

Hennessey was going on about some sort of exercise regimen and some schedule for him to check in on Eclipse's muscle tone, but most of that was just a bunch of doctor talk that Clint didn't really need to listen to. The biggest concern that had been on Clint's mind was put to rest the moment he got a good look into Eclipse's eyes.

Although the Darley Arabian wouldn't be coming along for this one, he would be there for plenty more rides after it.

"Do whatever you think you need to do, Doc," Clint said as he gave Hennessey a good-natured pat on the back. "I've got to catch a stage out of town."

"Really? Where are you headed?"

But Clint was already walking out of the stables. Glancing over his shoulder, he said, "If you need any payment before I get back, talk to Rick Hartman. He'll take care of you."

"Well, I guess that's fine then. Have a good trip."

It was odd gearing up and getting ready to leave without saddling up Eclipse in the process. On the other hand, looking over the shoulder of a few prisoners and some overly cautious US Marshals wasn't exactly the type of thing that required a fast set of legs.

In fact, the more Clint thought about the job he'd taken, the more he wondered why he'd agreed to take it. Even before that thought finished crossing his mind, Clint already had his answer.

Even The Gunsmith needed to work for a living. Besides, it never hurt to have the US Marshals owe him a favor.

All in all, Clint figured the job would be worth all the boredom of tailing a couple chained men on a train. After that, he just might be able to look in on a few old friends in Tombstone.

By the time the job was over, he might just have to go looking for some real excitement.

NINE

It was another day in hell.

The men who lived in the prison with no name woke up after a particularly restless night. There was plenty of excitement in the air as well as a couple of visitors touring the place.

For the most part, the visitors just paced up and down the aisle between the two rows of cells. They glared in at the prisoners like they were caged animals who didn't know what the hell was going on, but that was nothing new.

Inside the cells, the prisoners remained curled up on their beds or sitting with their heads hanging low. Long, greasy hair hung in front of dirty faces like a matted curtain and rotting teeth remained hidden behind grimy faces. Still, even though none of them spoke, every one of the prisoners knew more about what was going on than any clean-shaven visitor.

The single door leading into the prison was open, but a burly man with a shotgun stood there to block it. Hardly any sunlight made it past the imposing figure and the rest merely curled around him as though even it was thinking twice about entering the dusty hole.

Two more armed men walked along the single path

leading to the back of the squat building while several more waited outside. Not all of those armed men were strangers, however. A few of them were guards that were just as familiar to the prisoners as the scratches on the walls. At the moment, even those guards didn't seem too happy about the men who'd arrived less than an hour ago.

One of those strangers was a lanky fellow wearing a black suit and matching waistcoat. The only parts of him that stood out in the shadowy prison were the gold watch chain crossing his belly, the gun in his hand and the fire in his eyes. What little bit of his face that wasn't in shadow thanks to his hat was covered in a brushy mustache that came down well past his bottom lip.

"So you haven't seen this other guard for how long?" the shadowy man asked.

The normal prison guard had been standing in the back, doing his best to keep out of everyone else's way. Despite the fact that he was nearly twice the size of the man in black, he still fidgeted a bit before answering the question.

"I saw him yesterday," the guard said.

"And when should you have seen him again?"

The guard paused when he noticed that all the prisoners were looking in his direction. They could smell his uneasiness like a wolf could smell blood in the air.

The shadowy man stepped forward so suddenly that his coat flew open and the US Marshal badge pinned there caught a stray beam of sunlight. "I'm the one asking the questions," the Marshal said. "Look at me, not them."

When the guard turned to look at the Marshal, he straightened up for a moment. Only a moment. Then, he backed right down again and tried to ignore the smirks showing up inside the various cages.

"I should've seen him when I got here this morning," the guard said.

"And you didn't see him?"

"No, Marshal Kelso. Not a trace of him."

"And you say he's not the type of man to desert his post?"

The guard shook his head. "No sir. He liked his job."

Marshal Kelso walked straight down the middle of the aisle, his eyes darting back and forth to fix upon each and every prisoner in turn. He stopped when he got in between Trask's and Redwater's cells. His hand lowered to hover over the gun at his side.

"What about these two?" Kelso asked. "Have they been doing anything odd lately?"

Before the guard could answer, Trask lifted his head to stare straight at the lawman. "Oh, no sir," Trask sneered. "We just been behaving real nicely all locked up in here."

Marshal Kelso squared off so he could look directly into Trask's cell.

"And as for ol' Smitty, he sure did like his job," Trask said. "He just loved coming in here and waking us up at all hours. You ask me, he's probably off somewhere right now getting his talliwacker shined because that's what he really needed. Maybe if he finally does get himself some pussy, he'll act a bit more civilized."

Kelso's face remained impassive, although his eyes did narrow slightly as Trask went on.

"You want to stare us down, go ahead, Marshal. And as for Smitty, I hope he gets himself fucked real good. And that goes the same for you."

"Guard," Kelso said without taking his eyes off of Trask. "Unlock these cells so we can get these two pieces of shit out of here."

The guard stepped forward and sifted through the keys on the ring he carried. "But, uh, what about Smitty?"

"We're here for these two prisoners. If he abandoned his post, he should just be real happy that all the prisoners are present and accounted for. My advice to you is to tell him to find another job the next time you see him."

"And . . . what if I don't see him?"

"Well, then," Kelso said as he stepped aside to let the guard unlock the cell door. "That would be your problem, wouldn't it?"

The guard gritted his teeth as he turned the key in the lock and pulled open the cell door. "I guess so," was all he said before standing aside and letting the Marshal take over from there.

Already, two other Marshals were walking toward the cells with their shotguns leveled at the prisoners. One of them was a man with a dark, olive complexion and a meticulously groomed mustache that looked more as though it had been drawn onto his upper lip. The other man was slender and slightly below average height. Although his age didn't show too much in his face or eyes, it came through just fine in his gray beard and salt-and-pepper hair.

"Put those shackles on him, Ed," Kelso said.

When he stepped into the light streaming in through Trask's brick-sized window, Ed Rivera's face could be seen in better detail. His features were distinctly Spanish and his skin had the color of desert sand.

The Spaniard handed his shotgun to Kelso and took hold of the shackles that had been draped over the back of his neck.

"Hold your arms out," Rivera said in a voice touched by a Castilian accent. "And spread your legs."

Trask did as he was told, lathering a slimy grin onto his face as Rivera clamped the iron bracelets around his wrists and then knelt to shackle his ankles.

"Ohh, you look good down there, boy," Trask said.

The shotgun's hammers snapped back and Kelso lifted it so both barrels pointed straight at Trask's face. "Shut your hole before I save the judge a whole lot of trouble."

Trask fell silent, but kept the smirk on his face as Rivera attached the shackles to his ankles. The irons on his arms and legs were connected by a thick length of chain which was long enough for Trask to stand up, but not straighten his back.

Rivera took hold of Trask by the shoulder and shoved him out of the cell. Trask might have fallen flat on his face if he hadn't been so accustomed to walking in chains. He did stumble, but managed to stop before he bumped against the barrel of Marshal Kelso's shotgun.

Keeping the shotgun in place, Kelso handed Rivera his gun. "Now for the other one."

The guard was already unlocking Redwater's cell. When the key clicked into place, he turned it and stepped aside before the door even started to swing open. Redwater had the most fearsome reputation of any prisoner that ever spent a day in any of those cells. Every guard knew about it. Every prisoner knew about it and apparently the Marshals knew about it too.

"You going to give us any trouble?" Kelso asked.

Trask started to say something, but was silenced as Rivera shoved him roughly toward the prison door.

In his cell, Redwater sat with his head hanging low and his hands dangling off of his knees. He let the Marshal's question settle in the air before slowly shaking his head.

Kelso reached out to open the door with one hand while keeping his other hand wrapped around the shotgun he'd been given. The door swung on its rusty hinges, making a rusty squeak that sounded like a cat being gutted alive. It barely opened halfway before it stopped on its own.

At the sound of Rivera's footsteps returning, Kelso reached his free hand back toward the Spaniard. Rivera draped another set of shackles over Kelso's arm and stepped so he could aim his shotgun through the Indian's bars.

Tossing the shackles into the cell, Kelso said, "Put them on."

Redwater lifted himself up from the edge of his cot and

stepped over to where the shackles had landed. Even though he was out of arm's reach from the bars, all of the lawmen twitched when Redwater made a quick little move toward the door.

To Redwater, the shift of his lips was a grin. To anyone else looking on, it might have been a subtle snarl.

"Don't make me ask again," Kelso said.

Sure enough, Redwater reached down and scooped up the shackles in his callused hand. First he snapped two of them onto his ankles and then he snapped one onto each wrist. It wasn't the easiest maneuver to pull off, but he'd had plenty of practice.

"Good," Kelso said while nudging the cell door the rest of the way open with his shotgun. "Now let's get moving."

Redwater took slow, shuffling steps toward the door and had to bow his head in order to get through. Although it was barely recognizable, he flinched ever so slightly when the guard reached behind him to shut the cell door. When he saw that nobody was going into that cell after him, Redwater turned his back on the cage and walked along with the Marshals.

If nobody was going to check over his cell, Redwater knew that Smitty wouldn't be seen again for some time.

It wouldn't have taken much to find the missing guard's body along with the razor sharp pocket knife that had been used to hack it into pieces. All that was required was a bit of digging beneath Redwater's cot and a real strong stomach.

TEN

The train was late in pulling away from the station, but Clint wasn't about to complain. He was just happy to be on it, since that meant he was that much closer to finishing the job. When he'd been approached by the US Marshals' office, Clint thought the job sounded like it was something that he wouldn't mind doing.

Now, looking back on the conversation and what seemed to be ahead of him, Clint figured the man who'd sold him on the job was just one hell of a fast talker. The more he thought about it, the more the job seemed like glorified babysitting duty.

Well, at least he would still be able to get to Tombstone and do some visiting while the US Marshals paid for the ticket.

The train was still barely moving as Clint made his way through one passenger car and then another in his search for a good seat. As per his instructions, Clint stepped into the next car, found a seat and waited. After a few minutes had gone by, the adjoining door opened once again and a burly man wearing a double shoulder rig stepped inside. The man was about Clint's height, but with a frame that sported several more layers of thick muscle. His skin was dark as smoke and piercing eyes stared out from beneath a simple brown hat.

In no time at all, the black man picked out where Clint was sitting and walked straight over to him. The car was relatively empty, so there wasn't anyone else but Clint sitting in the short row of seats toward the front of the car.

"You'd be Clint Adams?" the black man asked.

Clint nodded. "Yes, I would."

After another quick study, the black man nodded as though he could instantly tell the truth in Clint's words. With that, a smile appeared on his face that was friendly while still managing to be a little intimidating. "Ike Samuels," he said, holding out a thick hand.

Clint shook it and could feel that the other man wasn't putting even half of his strength into the grip. "Pleased to meet you, Ike. Are you one of the Marshals?"

"Not officially, but I work with them enough to earn my own badge. There's a few too many good ol' boys in the Marshals to let someone like me in with them."

"So how'd you wind up on an assignment like this?" Clint asked. "I'm still trying to figure out why I signed up."

Ike grinned at the way Clint delivered that line and relaxed a bit into his seat. "I worked for eight years as a guard in one of the worst prisons in the country. When it comes to handling prisoners, you might say I got a knack." Leaning in so he could nudge Clint with his elbow, Ike added, "it does me good to see some of these white boys in chains for a change."

Although Clint couldn't help but laugh out loud at Ike's wisecrack, he knew it might have been a joke like that which had kept him out of the Marshals. Some of those lawmen weren't exactly known for their sense of humor.

"Well, look at it this way," Clint said. "Marshals come and go, but quality freelancers are always in demand."

"No need to tell it to me. Don't let none of the others

know about this, but I pull down more pay than everyone but the man in charge of this job."

The train lurched once more as the whistle started wailing outside. Apparently, the last of the stragglers had been let on board and the engineer was finally pushing the throttle forward. Clint looked out the window and saw the last couple inches of the station's platform slip away.

"Looks like we're on our way," Clint said.

Ike nodded and kept quiet as another passenger walked by on their way to another car that was serving drinks. Once the immediate area was clear once again, he looked back to Clint and said, "I don't mind talking to you, Clint, but I should get down to business and get back to my own job."

"Understood. Go right ahead."

"There's five of us on this train. Me, two Marshals and two prisoners. Rivera is the Spanish fella and he's been in the Marshals for a few years. Bob Kelso is the Marshal in charge and he's earned his spot. There were more Marshals on the way here and there'll be more to meet us at Tombstone, but the group on the train is small enough to keep things moving along quickly."

Clint nodded. Now he could see that the Marshal who'd approached him about the job hadn't been overstating how important Clint's role would be.

"As for the prisoners," Ike continued. "There's only two of them, but they killed enough men to pay for a dozen folk's trip to hell. Only problem is that they're real good at covering their tracks, so no court could get them hung. They're also bad enough that no vigilantes want to risk getting close to them."

"Interesting predicament."

"That's one way of putting it," Ike said. "I call it holding on to a losing hand. It's gotten to the point where killing these two is almost like bad luck or something. At least there's one judge with the gumption to lock these animals away where nobody will ever see them again."

"How'd the transfer go at the old prison?"

Ike pulled in a deep breath and let it out in a troubled sigh. "It went as good as can be expected."

"But, what else?"

"What else is that one of the guards came up missing just before we got there."

"What?"

"They were short one guard," Ike said. "And I'd bet money that one of them two killed him. If I had to place a wager, I'd put it on the Indian. He was shifting around in his cell and the other one was a little too noisy. Kind of like he was trying to draw attention to himself."

"And nobody followed up on it?" Clint asked.

"Kelso knew something was wrong, but he wanted to get them two out of there before anything else happened. "Much as I would have liked to catch them in a hanging crime, I'd have to say that I agree with the Marshal. Holding on to these two is like holding a couple snakes by the tail. You just know one or both of 'em are waiting to snap back and bite you."

"Well, I'm here to do my part. What do you want me to do?"

"Did you see which compartment we're in?"

Clint nodded.

"Just walk by there every so often and one of us will signal that we're all right with a nod. If something's wrong, we'll shake our head."

"Easy enough to remember. What about a back-up signal in case something is very wrong?"

Ike thought about that for a moment and said, "if everything's gone to hell or it's headed that way, we'll knock on the walls or try to make some kind of noise. If we can't even do that much, then you probably won't even be able to see or hear us at all."

"And then I'll know for myself that things are headed south."

"Exactly." Ike got up and slid his hat onto the back of his head. If it wasn't for the gun around his waist, he might have looked like a rancher or farmer who'd stopped by to shoot the breeze. The easy smile on his face certainly didn't give away the fact that he was in charge of two bloodthirsty animals.

"I'll be seeing you, Clint."

Clint nodded. "Count on it."

ELEVEN

No matter how much someone said, there was always something more to know. Clint didn't have any doubt that Ike was being up front with him, but there was still something else that maybe even Ike didn't know. Clint could feel it like a storm that was just over the horizon. Ike could probably feel it too, but there wasn't much use in sitting around and swapping speculations.

Since he was officially on the job, Clint decided to get out of his seat and start acting like it. As he walked down the middle of the car, he nodded to the few passengers who looked up at him and sidled past the rest. Something nagged at him, just as it had since he'd first been given the assignment.

Suddenly, with his hand upon the latch of the door leading out of the car, Clint realized what it was that had been bothering him.

Two killers who could make people disappear like they never even existed. One of them a wiry fellow and the other a big Indian.

David Trask and John Redwater.

The names hit Clint and this time, they stuck. He'd heard them before, but they hadn't done anything but dig under his skin like a couple of burrowing insects. Now, however, the flag finally went up and Clint knew that he'd heard of those two before.

They were both wanted in several states for robbing and kidnapping, although Clint couldn't recall whether or not they were wanted for the same crimes. One thing that he knew for certain was that robbers and kidnappers didn't work alone. Jobs like those required a gang and if they were still out there, the chance of them coming to free one or both of the prisoners was pretty good.

Trying to break them out of a prison was one thing, but snatching them out of a train or somewhere else along the line was something else.

Clint was a man who followed his instincts and now he was very glad of that. Despite everything else, his instincts had told him to take the job offered by the Marshals. Now he knew why. The lawmen would need every last bit of help they could get.

The train was picking up steam and starting to move quickly along its way. The tracks were rattling beneath it in a steady rhythm, which Clint had always found soothing. As it acquired more speed, the train even started to rock gently back and forth. The sound of the engine faded into the background like the constant flow of wind.

Feeling a renewed urgency, Clint decided to walk the length of the train and see if he might be able to spot any familiar faces. Even if he couldn't recognize any wanted men, he figured he could at least pick up on someone that might be up to no good.

He stepped from one car into another, putting the prisoners' compartment even farther behind him. When he reached out to open the next door, the handle turned on its own and the door swung open directly in front of him.

Clint pulled back with a start, but whatever surprise he might have felt was doubled upon the face of the man who'd gotten to the door before him.

"Oh, excuse me," a shorter fellow with bright red hair said. From there, he stepped aside and let Clint pass before hustling off to the car Clint had just left behind.

For the moment, that car wasn't too full, but that would change before too much longer. Clint recognized one face that had been in the car with him when he was talking to Ike, but none of the others jumped out at him for any reason. Still nodding to faces as he walked by, Clint moved on to the next car in line.

His hand reached out automatically to open the door, but came up short when the door wouldn't budge. Before he tried it again, he realized he was trying to walk into a car used for baggage and anything else the train might have been hauling.

Clint took a quick look into the car, but couldn't see much through the thickly smoked glass. Taking a step away from the door, he paused between cars to fill his lungs with a few breaths of fresh air.

Just when he figured he'd spent enough time outside, Clint realized that his timing couldn't have been better. In fact, he spent just long enough on the rickety grating to make the men hiding inside the baggage car think that he'd already called it quits and left entirely.

TWELVE

The instant Clint heard the hushed voices from inside the baggage car, he froze in his spot.

His heart stood still for a few moments as he held his breath and waited to make sure that what he'd heard hadn't been a rustle of wind or something shifting within the next car.

With his ears straining to their limits, Clint didn't have to wait long to realize that he'd heard correctly. The sound he'd heard was indeed a voice and it had most definitely come from the next car. He couldn't make out what was being said, but the sound of another person's voice became distinct enough to raise the hackles on the back of Clint's neck.

Slowly lowering himself as much as he could without moving his feet, Clint did the best he could to keep out of sight if someone else tried looking through the narrow window on the door. Even though the glass was smoked to obscure the view, Clint would have stood out just fine against the background of the sky.

Instinctively, Clint's hand lowered until his fingers brushed against the leather of his holster. The weight of the modified Colt was present at his side, like the reassuring feel of a hand on his shoulder.

The voices came once more from the inside of the car. Whoever was speaking had to have been close to the door in the first place for Clint to hear them at all over the clatter of the wheels against the tracks. This time, however, the other person was so close that Clint could make out their silhouette through the smoked glass window.

". . . out there?" was all Clint could hear through the door.

There were a few more voices as the silhouette stopped moving behind the glass.

Clint swore the person on the other side of that glass had seen him. He couldn't make out any details or even a face, but Clint still swore that whatever eyes were behind that glass were now focused squarely on him.

Still, Clint kept his faith in his gun hand and held his ground. He figured that the smoked glass would work for him in this situation just so long as he kept perfectly still.

As he concentrated on playing the part of a statue, Clint focused in on any little bit of information his senses could gather. Judging by the sounds he heard, there were at least three men inside that car. Since nobody had said anything or simply opened the door to take a look outside, Clint figured that those men in there didn't want to be found.

After a while of standing there planted in one spot, Clint started to feel less like a statue and more like a sitting duck. Now that he was certain the men in the next car weren't porters, he was starting to wonder why he was about to let them get in the first shot.

Moments before his reflexes took over, Clint heard another round of grumbling coming from inside the baggage car. After that, the blurry silhouette moved away from the glass.

Clint let out the breath he'd been holding, but didn't allow himself to relax. One advantage for sitting still over the last minute or two was that he'd been able to come up with a good plan of action. Now, it was time to put that plan into motion.

Stepping on the balls of his feet, Clint kept low enough so that he wouldn't be seen immediately through the window. When he got close enough to the car, he reached out and placed one hand against the wall beside the door. He leaned forward on that hand, which allowed him to ease up to the door slowly and quietly.

Inside, the voices were getting a little louder. Apparently, they were under the impression that they were alone. They let their guard down so much, in fact, that Clint could even start to pick out bits and pieces of their conversation.

". . . out there," one of the voices said from within the car.

The response to that came from a source much closer to the door. "I looked myself, didn't I? There ain't no one out there."

". . . can you be so certain?" This was a third voice and it seemed to be coming from somewhere between the other two.

"I can be certain because I just looked through the goddamn window myself. Can we just get on with this?"

"Well, it's . . . around here somewhere."

". . . ain't in this car. We know he said . . . anywhere on the train."

Clint was taking more and more interest in the conversation. Being careful not to move too quickly, he eased a shoulder against the door and then set one ear against it as well. Letting out his breath, he focused on whatever he could hear being said inside the car.

"We'll just have to keep looking," the voice in the middle said. "The train just left, so we got plenty of time."

"But we can't wait till we get to Tombstone," replied the farthest voice from the door. "There'll just be more guards waiting there. We got to get . . . off of . . . before it stops."

"What about the Marshals that are already on board?"

the closest voice asked. "They'll probably be on the look-out for anything peculiar."

"If one of them looks too close in the wrong direction, we'll just have to take them down. We knew it might come to that."

Clint didn't have to hear another word. He moved his head away from the door and shifted his feet so that his shoulders were lined up against it at a ninety degree angle. His whole body followed so one side was pressed against the door while both feet braced against the floorboards.

With every one of his muscles coiled and ready to spring, Clint steadied his breathing and let a few moments pass until the right one presented itself.

Inside, the men were still talking. By the sound of it, they were also starting to pace around while pushing over whatever cargo they could get their hands on.

"We know he's on this train," one of them said. "We all saw him and them Marshals get on."

"You sure that means the rest was true?"

"He's got no reason to lie. If'n he did, then we'll make this thing bloodier than even he could imagine."

Clint's moment presented itself. He felt it as clearly as if it had been marked by a signal fire. When it came, he made his move.

He reached out one hand and knocked.

THIRTEEN

"What was that?"

Clint couldn't tell which of the three voices had said that, but at this point it didn't matter. All of the sets of footsteps had either stopped entirely or were headed toward the door. He listened intently to each and every sound, preparing himself for one sound in particular.

The footsteps that got closest to the door came to a stop. There were a few hurried whispers and then the rattle of the door's latch being lifted.

That was the sound Clint had been waiting for and when it came, he acted like a trap that had been sprung.

With every bit of strength he'd been saving up, Clint pushed with both feet against the floor and shoved his shoulder hard against the door. Since the latch was already lifted, the door came open easily and all of Clint's force slammed the door against the man inside who'd been opening it.

The edge of the door caught the man on the other side along the center line of his entire body. From his gut, up to his ribs and then square against his nose and chin, the impact sent so much pain through him at once that he went numb almost immediately.

Not that the man would appreciate it much, of course. He was too busy trying to break his fall as he toppled back against stacks of cargo that filled most of the car.

Clint was still riding his own momentum as he slid against the swinging door and rolled into the car. Although he did his best to look where he was going, there wasn't much of a way for him to know what was inside the car until he was already there. He felt a crate directly in front of him and was just able to stop himself before rolling straight into it.

The other men inside the car were just as surprised as the one who'd taken the door in his face. By the time Clint was able to right himself and get his bearings, they'd already done the same.

One of the men in front of Clint had backed himself against a stack of something covered by a tarp. He wore a red bandanna around his neck and was already grabbing for a rifle that had been propped against the tarp. "Who the hell is that?" he grunted.

"It don't matter who he is," replied the man at the farthest end of the car. This one had a round face covered by a thick layer of whiskers. He'd already drawn his pistol and was lowering himself to one knee. "Just kill him!"

The bearded man was already kneeling down in a firing position and was reaching for a gun at his side. There was no mistaking the bad intentions in his eyes or what he would do once he got his hand on his gun.

Clint wasn't about to wait to see what the bearded man's reasons were. He was reacting on pure instinct and with nothing more than a thought, his hand was filled by his own modified Colt. Clint cleared leather and brought the gun up to aim with a flicker of motion. In the next instant, he was squeezing the trigger.

The inside of the train car filled with the thunder of gunfire as Clint's Colt spat out a tongue of flame and shot its lead through the air. Although the bearded man's one-knee stance had done well in making him a smaller target, it also caused him to take Clint's bullet squarely in his kneecap.

Leaning back and dropping his gun, the bearded man tried to let out a howl of pain, but couldn't get out anything but a tense grunt. His kneecap had shattered and the bullet was lodged in between the bones, turning his entire world into a river of pain.

Clint tipped himself forward so he could move between two stacks of baggage. With the train moving along at a healthy pace, the car and everything inside of it was shifting back and forth to the rhythm of the motion. Clint thought he was going to be off-balance, but was able to steady himself at the last moment.

He came to a stop just short of the side of the car and quickly turned so his back was against the wall.

"You all right?" one of the men shouted to the other.

After another grunt, the bearded man hollered, "I got shot in the kneecap! What the hell do you think?"

Clint tried to get a better look around now that he was inside the car itself. Before he could see much of anything, however, the man with the red bandanna was stepping up directly in front of him.

Even before he planted his feet, the man with the bandanna held his rifle at hip level and fired off a shot. The bullet punched a hole through the side of the car a few inches from Clint's shoulder and was soon followed by the sound of another round being levered into the chamber.

Rather than take another shot, Clint lowered his head and charged the man in front of him. He buried his shoulder into that man's gut before the rifle was reloaded. Clint could hear the air rush from the man's lungs, but could tell that the rifle was still firmly in his grip.

Clint caught a glimpse of motion coming from the side

of the car where the door was still swinging on its hinges. All he needed to see was a man with blood streaming down his face stepping up and reaching for the gun at his side.

Shifting his stance, Clint squared his shoulders and faced off against the man who'd caught the door in his face when Clint had first arrived. Unfortunately, the man with the bandanna was standing between them and blocking most of their view.

Clint was still holding the Colt and he brought it up and around so he could clear the other man's body. In order to keep from getting snagged on the human barrier, Clint had to swing his arm out a bit before centering his aim.

When his arm came to a stop, Clint was holding the Colt sideways with the knuckles of his gun hand facing up. Since adjusting his hand would have taken another precious few fractions of a second, he did the best he could and squeezed off a shot.

The Colt roared in his hand and though its bullet didn't hit its mark, it came close enough to send the man with the broken nose diving for cover.

Before Clint could forget about the man less than an inch away from him, he was reminded by a sharp knee to his stomach. The fellow with the rifle delivered his blow and stepped back, pulling his gun in close so he could take another shot.

Clint knew he had less than a second to react and did so by taking hold of the rifle's barrel and shoving it upward. He let go just as the trigger was pulled and a shot was drilled through the roof of the car. Clint followed up with a swing from his other hand, delivering the side of his Colt straight to the man's temple.

The Colt bounced off the man's skull with a dull thud, sending that one's eyes rolling up into his head. He keeled right over and took his rifle with him, landing in a pile upon the floor.

"All right," Clint said as he looked around at the three men, "what the hell are you up to?"

Clint glanced at each of the men in turn. The one who'd been shot in the kneecap appeared to have passed out from the pain, but was still breathing like a dog having a strenuous dream. The man with the bandanna was slouched against a crate, blinking furiously to try and come back to his senses.

That just left the one with the bloody nose and bruised face. He was staring at Clint from the spot where he'd landed after ducking for cover. Clint's eyes focused on him since it seemed that he was the one most likely to give an answer.

"Well?" Clint asked.

The man with the bloody nose paused for a second and then started laughing. That laughter was almost enough to cover up the sound of footsteps rushing out from somewhere in the car and behind Clint.

That's when Clint realized that there was at least one more man that had remained silent and hidden this entire time.

Swearing under his breath, Clint spun around and was just in time to see a skinny fellow with sunken features rushing toward him with a knife. The blade was clenched in a tight fist and cocked back close to the skinny fellow's ear.

By the time Clint had turned all the way around, the skinny fellow had closed the distance between them and was bringing his blade down in a quick, stabbing motion. Those sunken eyes turned wide in expectation of his kill and his teeth bared as the blade was brought down toward its target.

Clint blinked while the Colt barked once from its spot in his hand. The gun was brought around and aimed like it was an extension of Clint's own arm. It fired with no more than a thought from its wielder and blasted a hole clean through the skinny fellow's body like a rock that had been tossed through wet newspaper.

With the smoke hanging heavy in the air, Clint turned around and brought his gun to bear on the man with the broken nose. The glare on his face was more than enough to freeze the man where he stood. The smoking Colt was enough to get him to drop his own weapon and stumble against the door.

"Start talking," Clint said.

FOURTEEN

Trask and Redwater sat with their hands cuffed behind their backs, their ankles chained together and a single chain looped through their bindings and locked around the most solid post in the compartment. So far, Trask had been doing all of the talking and even that wasn't more than a few words. Redwater merely stared straight ahead as though he could see through everything and everybody.

Rivera sat at the back of the compartment, facing the prisoners with his shotgun nearby.

Kelso sat at the front of the car with his pistol holstered and an additional shotgun behind his back.

Ike stood at the door so he could hear what was going on in the hall as well as see anything that happened inside.

Between all that coverage, it was no wonder that the prisoners were in no mood to talk.

At one point, Trask's ears perked up and he lifted his face as though he'd just picked up an enticing scent. "What was that?" he asked.

None of the lawmen so much as twitched in response to the question.

But Trask still looked around. "Did you hear that?"

A few moments later, Rivera's eyes narrowed and he sat

up. He reflexively brought up the shotgun with his thumb
resting across the hammers.

Marshal Kelso glanced over to him. "What's the matter,
Rivera?"

"I think I did hear something," he replied, leaning
toward the wall of the compartment that separated the passengers from the outside of the train. "Could have been
gunshots."

Before either of the other two guards could respond, a
faint pop could be heard. For the most part, it was muffled
by the sound of the wheels clattering against the tracks.
Even so, enough of the sound drifted into the compartment
to raise some suspicions.

Another few moments ticked by while everyone else in
the compartment started looking toward Marshal Kelso for
guidance about what to do next. Ike and Rivera waited ex-
pectantly for orders. Trask and Redwater looked as if they
were sitting in the front row of a play.

Finally, Kelso reached behind him to grab his shotgun
and said, "Rivera, I want you to go and check it out. That
noise couldn't have come from too far away or we wouldn't
have even heard it."

What bothered Kelso more than anything was that he
wasn't even sure if they would have heard it anyhow if
Trask hadn't drawn attention to it first. Still, when staring
into the eyes of a cornered wolf, the last thing he wanted to
do was show any sign of fear of wariness.

Either one of those things meant weakness.

And weakness meant death.

Rivera stood up and pointed the shotgun at both prisoners. He kept the gun aimed in their direction as he moved
in front of them and headed for the door. Ike was already
stepping aside, aiming his gun at the prisoners as well and
letting Rivera step out of the compartment without letting
his guard down in the slightest.

Ike shut the door behind the Marshal and stood with one

heel against it so he could tell the moment it moved again without having to take his eyes off of the prisoners.

Throughout this entire process, Trask rocked slightly in his seat with his hands clenching and unclenching. His eyes were so intently focused on the lawmen that he didn't remember to blink until Rivera was gone and the door was shut behind him.

Redwater, on the other hand, remained in the same spot he had been since he'd been shoved into the compartment. Only the Indian's eyes moved as he watched every last detail of what was going on around him.

"Might as well sit tight, you two," Marshal Kelso said. "Even if this train burns down around us, you won't be moving from those seats you're in right now. In fact, if I were you, I'd pray to God that nothing happened to this train."

Redwater blinked once. When his eyes opened, they were focused on the same spot directly in front of him. By this time, it wouldn't have seemed odd if two wisps of smoke started to curl out of the points on the wall where those eyes were staring.

Trask leaned back in his seat, but didn't relax the fists he'd been making. "We'll just see about all that, Marshal. We'll just see."

FIFTEEN

The neatly stacked crates and baggage in the luggage car had already been toppled and messed up thanks to the scuffle that had recently ended. Now, thanks to Clint's guidance, that mess had just gotten a little worse.

Not only were there bodies laying on the floor, but Clint had ordered the one remaining gunman who was still awake to strip whatever rope or twine he could find from the boxes to use to tie the hands of his partners. After his most recent turn of bad luck, the gunman wasn't inclined to put up much resistance to those orders.

As the gunman moved about his task, Clint kept his gun drawn and spoke in a level, commanding voice.

"What were you men doing here?" Clint asked.

The gunman tried to scowl, but his face was already so battered and bruised that the expression only brought him another jolt of pain from where the door had slammed into his nose. Now that he knew trying to look tough was a hopeless cause, the gunman balled up his fist and slammed it against the nearest crate in frustration. When he looked back at Clint, he seemed more like an agitated youngster.

"We came here for the money," the gunman said.

Clint looked around at the stacks of boxes and luggage piled about the car. "What money?"

"The money being guarded by them Marshals. There's a whole mess of it and maybe even some gold as well."

"What's all this money and gold doing on board?"

"Hell if I know. We don't even care. All we care about is that it's us that're leaving the train with it all."

"All right, then," Clint said. "Where is this money supposed to be?"

"It's stored somewhere in here or in the next car up. We already checked that other car, so we came here."

"And you didn't find anything?"

Once again, the gunman sneered. This time, however, the pain didn't bother him so much. He was either getting used to it or it just didn't seem so bad anymore when compared to everything else that had happened. "No," he grunted. "We didn't find much of anything."

"Funny that all this money and gold is supposed to be way up here when the Marshals are back in another part of the train." Clint said that almost more to himself than anyone else who might be listening. His eyes were still on the gunman, however, which allowed him to pick up on something very important.

"Yeah," the gunman said as if he'd only just thought about that aspect. "That is kinda strange." Pondering that a little more led the gunman to a thoughtful scowl. That, in turn, led to a wince of pain that brought the frustration roaring back into him like a stampede.

Suddenly, Clint heard the sound of a door being pushed open and heavy footsteps knocking against the balconies connecting the two cars. Taking a quick step to one side, Clint faced the door that was still swinging against the frame while also keeping the gunman with the broken nose in his sight.

A hand reached out to push the door open, which soon

revealed the face of one of the Marshals that had just been
a topic of conversation. Clint lowered his gun and waited
for the lawman to step into the car and get a look at what
was left of the would-be robbers.

"What's going on here?" Rivera asked.

"Not a lot at the moment," Clint said lightly. "You missed
all the fun."

Rivera's eyes darted back and forth, but the shotgun in
his hands stayed up and ready to fire. "Yeah. I guess I did."
Positioning himself with his back to an empty corner,
Rivera planted his feet and said, "I better get an answer
quick or I'll just have to come up with one on my own."

Clint nudged the gunman with the toe of his boot. "Go
on and tell the man what you told me."

Grudgingly, the gunman spilled the whole story once
more for the Marshal's sake. He took a few more liberties
than the first time around to make sure to cast Clint in a bad
light, but none of the exaggerations were much of a surprise to anyone used to dealing with prisoners. When he
was done, the gunman was cringing and holding his broken
nose. When he saw that he wasn't getting any sympathy
from the lawman, the look of frustration returned.

"Is that what happened?" Rivera asked while looking
over to Clint.

"Except for the part about me busting in here and gun-
ning everyone down like a mad dog, it's pretty close."

"What about this money he was talking about?"

"That's the interesting part," Clint replied. "It's also the
part that doesn't hold up. In fact, it would take a real idiot
to think that all the badges and guns would be guarding a
passenger car when there's a stash of money hiding with
the carpetbags."

"Hey!" the gunman snarled. He was cut short before he
could get anything else out by a stab of pain that brought
both hands up to his bloody face.

Both Clint and Rivera ignored the other man as they started glancing at the mess inside the car.

"Well, we should make sure these men won't be going anywhere when they wake up." Nodding toward the skinny fellow who'd swung the knife, Rivera added, "Except for him. It doesn't look like he'll be going anywhere. As for the rest, they need to be locked up. Here," the Marshal said after reaching behind his back and pulling out a pair of handcuffs. "Put these on that one over there. Looks like he's starting to wake up."

Clint glanced to where Rivera was looking and saw that the gunman with the red bandanna was indeed starting to squirm on the floor. He took the handcuffs that were handed to him and walked over to lock them around the gunman's wrists before the guy remembered where he was.

"Here," Rivera said as he took out another set of cuffs and tossed them over to the man with the broken nose. "You can put these on yourself."

Although the gunman did his level best to appear menacing, his broken face just wasn't cutting it. Even as he tried to put up some sort of fuss, he still wound up taking the cuffs and locking them around his own wrists. It took him a few tries, but he still managed to get them on just fine.

"That just leaves him," Rivera said, nodding to where the man with the beard was laying.

That one's face appeared unusually tranquil considering that his legs were stuck to the floor by a thick layer of blood. The wound in his knee was still oozing blood and his pants leg was black with all of it that had soaked into the material.

"I doubt he'll be waking up anytime soon," Clint said. "Even if he did, it's not like he would be running off anywhere."

Rivera nodded. "Good point. Still, I'll have someone sent back to see to him."

"Speaking of that," Clint said, "Are you the only ones who heard the shooting?"

"Probably not. We're just the only ones who recognized the sound over all the other ruckus."

Before Clint could say anything else, Rivera was walking forward and sticking his shotgun directly under the chin of the man with the broken nose. "Now, you need to tell me who put you up to this."

The gunman winced and started to form a profanity, but thought twice when the shotgun was pushed even harder against his chin.

Rivera recognized the fact that he was pushing against a deep bruise as well as a possible crack in the man's jaw. "Spill whatever you haven't told me, or I'll put you out of your misery real quick."

Clint was a good judge of men and could tell that Rivera wasn't about to pull that trigger. Still, it didn't seem that the gunman was so observant.

SIXTEEN

Although he was trying to be a hard case, the man with the broken nose wasn't able to hold up for very long before spelling out what few things he hadn't mentioned already. As Clint had suspected, the gunman didn't know about anything other than the money he was after. One thing he'd been holding on to the most was the name of the man who'd steered him toward that money in the first place.

"Eddie Vance," Clint said.

He was sitting with Marshal Kelso. Just over an hour had passed since he and Rivera had wrapped up the gunmen in the baggage car and everything was moving along normally. The train was rattling along its tracks and most of the passengers seemed no more than mildly curious about the lawmen walking through the cars.

"Eddie Vance?" Kelso repeated. He thought it over and then scowled as if he'd just accidentally swallowed a pinch of salt. "I heard the name, but it doesn't mean too much to me in this case. Isn't he mostly a stagecoach bandit?"

"As far as I know," Clint replied. "But he has been known to work some rather unsavory types. One of those unsavory types in particular has been rotting in a Texas prison for some time. That is, until just recently."

Kelso snapped his fingers and tensed up. "He used to run with Trask about seven or eight years ago."

Clint nodded. "They robbed a few payrolls, but it wasn't anything too big."

"Did you help track him down?"

"No. I've just had a bit of time to think about anything I've ever heard regarding Trask and his associates. It helps to keep up on such things when it's usually men like him that try to come after me."

"So those men you and Rivera found were sent here by Eddie Vance."

"Well, I'd say they were steered this way by Vance. The real concern is who told Vance to do the steering."

"And that would be Trask."

"Anything else would be a bit too much of a coincidence for my tastes. I'm not much of one for coincidences. There's also the question of whether or not there was a middleman between Eddie and Trask."

For a moment, it seemed as though Marshal Kelso wasn't going to say much of anything. He simply stared straight ahead. Finally, he closed his hand in a fist that made Clint think that the lawman was about to knock out a window.

"God damn that murdering son of a bitch," Kelso said under his breath.

A few of the passengers nearby turned to look at the lawman since they'd only caught a little bit of what Kelso had just said. They turned right back around again once Clint gave them a quick shrug.

"Well," Clint said, "it's not like you didn't expect something like this. I mean, this is why I was asked to tag along, wasn't it?"

"Yeah, but that still doesn't make it all right. Trask has been threatening to do harm to my men and once he hears that he got this close, I'll be forced to look at that smug grin he's always got on."

Clint paused before asking, "Who says he's got to know anything?"

Pulling in a deep breath, Marshal Kelso started to nod. The fire in his eyes died down a bit and was replaced by a vague semblance of a grin. "Good point. If he steered those men this way, it was probably for an escape. Either that, or a distraction. Was there any money in that car?"

Clint shook his head. "Nothing more than a few bits of jewelry scattered inside some of those bags. The crates were mostly dry goods and some mail bound for Tombstone."

"Then there's the answer. It was supposed to be a distraction."

"Actually, I was thinking the same thing. Unless there was some way for Trask to know the exact train he'd be on and everything being carried in that car, the rest had to be a bluff just to whet those robbers' appetites."

Now, Marshal Kelso wasn't just smirking, but he was starting to put on a smile that stretched from one ear to the other. "Those two prisoners have been on their best behavior for most of this ride. That is, apart from comments here and there. Apart from those threats, they've been like two well behaved kids."

"Probably just waiting for the opportunity that's supposed to be coming their way. I doubt those gunmen even knew Trask was on this train."

"Are you certain about that?"

Clint nodded. "Pretty certain. Those fellas went through too much to keep their loyalties to someone that threw them a lead to some pretend money and then let them charge into a gunfight."

"Then let's just keep this to ourselves," Kelso said. "No need letting my two guests know that we're on to them. We could use all the peace and quiet we can get. Speaking of which, I sure am looking forward to putting this whole job behind me. It's been a pain in the ass since it began."

"From what I recall about those two you've got in your custody, I don't have any trouble believing that."

"Well, if they think their little plans are moving along, they'll probably sit tight and wait for the fireworks to start. I'd say we've got at least an hour before they start to suspect anything."

"That depends on how convincing your deputy is when he's with them."

"Oh, I wouldn't worry about Rivera," Kelso said. "He made up some story about a fight breaking out between two passengers that knocked over a cabinet in another car. Judging by the disappointed looks on their faces, I'd say the prisoners bought it."

"So what would you like me to do?" Clint asked.

"Just sit tight for now. Try to relax. If anything happens, we both know how to contact the other. In the meantime, we'll all just keep our eyes and ears open and be ready to pounce at the first sign of trouble."

"Sounds good to me."

Kelso stood up and Clint followed his lead.

"You did a great job, Adams," Kelso said quietly. "I'm indebted to you."

With that, the Marshal turned and walked out of the car. Clint watched him go before sitting back down. Out of the corner of his eye, he noticed that one of the other passengers was watching him closer than any of the others.

In fact, that same passenger had been taking a keen interest in everything that went on between Clint and the lawman. After what had just happened, Clint knew better than to let that go unanswered.

SEVENTEEN

The boots fell solidly upon the floor as if the feet inside of them were trying to make holes as they walked by. The floor shook just a bit, but the floor had been shaking ever since the train had left the station. When the person walked by, his eyes seemed to graze over the occupants of the tables like a spotlight.

The glance was quick, but it shone brightly enough to make anyone look away until it passed.

As the steps headed for the door, the people in the nearby seats went back to their business. One of them, however, let out a slow, relieved breath.

The door opened and closed with the smack of wood against wood. That left only the conversation within the car and the constant rattle of wheels against the track to fill the air. That single relieved person took another quick glance toward the door and quickly pulled in the breath that had just been set free.

"Howdy," Clint said as he leaned against the door frame wearing a smile that was almost as bright as the gaze he'd cast upon the people he'd recently passed.

The woman sitting in a nearby seat tried to hide her surprise at first. Now, she played it up just a bit and held one hand flat against her collarbone. "You frightened me," she said.

Still smiling, Clint walked over to her and sat down. He took a quick look around and saw that everyone else in the car was paying more attention to their own conversations rather than anything else.

"And you were watching me," Clint replied.

The woman wore a simple dress made from pink cotton with white polka dots. The neckline dipped a little, but not enough to draw too much attention. It was cinched in tight around the middle, which did a good enough job of showing off her trim body and pert breasts. Her golden hair was tied back into a collection of large curls which wandered down just past her shoulders.

"Watching you?" she asked.

Clint nodded. "That's right. Ever since I walked in here, but mostly when I was over there talking to my friend."

"Well," she said, straightening up and meeting Clint's gaze levelly, "if you and your friend didn't want to attract some bit of attention, you shouldn't walk around wearing guns."

Clint didn't have to look down at the Colt holstered around his waist. Normally, the pistol's weight was noticed about as much as the weight of his arms dangling from their sockets. Just then, however, the gun was brought straight back to his attention.

"Fair enough," he said. Even though there was no edge in his voice, there was still a persistence in his eyes. Not a threat, but just an unapologetic way of looking at her without being shy about it.

"Why are you staring at me?" she asked while lowering her eyes a bit.

"Sorry. I'll bet someone as pretty as you gets used to men looking away when you glance in their direction."

The blonde turned her eyes completely away from Clint for a moment, but couldn't do a thing to hide the grin creeping onto her face. Taking a breath, she lifted her chin and fixed her eyes on him as though she meant to stare a hole through his head. That intensity lasted all of two seconds.

"All right, I was watching you," she said. "Is that a crime?"

"Not hardly. Although, I might be committing some sort of infraction for what's going through my head right now."

It was a move that could make Clint's day or bust him. This time, the gamble worked and the blonde had to lift her hand to cover her mouth as she started to laugh.

Clint tipped his hat and extended a hand. "My name's Clint Adams. Sorry if I startled you before."

The blonde put her hand in his and gave him a sweet smile when he clasped and shook it. "Heather Moore. And I deserved a little fright for watching you like I was about to rob you on your way out."

Clint dismissed that with a shrug. "I hope I'm not intruding here. Are you waiting for somebody?"

"Well, I wasn't supposed to be traveling alone. That's just how it worked out."

"Don't tell me someone had the nerve to let someone like you get away from them."

"Oh, nothing like that," Heather said. "I was supposed to be riding to Tombstone with my sister, but her husband fell ill and she had to stay behind. I didn't find out until the tickets were already bought and paid for. After a little bit of moping, I decided to take a trip and make the best of it."

"Then my next question is whether or not I stuck my foot in my mouth far enough already to make joining you inappropriate."

"Don't be silly. I don't mind the company. Since you're friends with a lawman, I suppose that means you can be trusted."

Clint paused for a moment as a rush of faces and situations went through his mind. For the most part, he found lawmen to be good men working hard at a nearly impossible job. But, as that rush of memory reminded him, not all lawmen were cut from the same cloth. Rather than shatter Heather's impression of them, Clint nodded and said, "You're a fine judge of character. At least, where I'm concerned."

Again, Heather laughed.

Every time she smiled was prettier than the last. As she became more accustomed to Clint's presence, she started leaning toward him a bit more until she was leaning up against him.

Clint kept the conversation light and even found himself enjoying it, right up until Heather tilted her head and said, "I heard there are some prisoners on board. Is that true?"

Hearing that brought Clint's defenses back up and added the slightest edge to his expression. Too bad there was still a job that needed to be done.

EIGHTEEN

Although it didn't take much to sidestep the question, Clint was uncomfortable that the prisoners were such common knowledge among everyone else on the train. Then again, it wasn't as if the US Marshals were doing too much to hide their presence. Kelso and the others may have been doing their best to keep quiet, but the shotguns in the deputies' hands weren't too hard to miss.

Leaving the car, Heather stepped away from the door leading to the next car and instead walked over to the narrow balcony spanning the two cars. She took hold of the railing which wasn't much more than a thin strip of metal and pulled in a lungful of the air that rushed by.

"I love traveling by train," she said. "It's so restful."

"It can be," Clint said.

"You mean when someone's not shooting at you?"

Clint looked over to her and got a sideways glance along with a smirk in return. Heather looked as though she was about to start laughing at any second.

"Isn't that what you gunfighters do?" she asked. "Go around shooting at each other like it was some kind of game?"

"Not if I can help it. I don't know what sort you usually

73

meet on these trains, but I don't like to think of myself as a gunfighter."

The fact that most everyone who'd heard of Clint Adams thought of him as a gunfighter wasn't the point. Just then, Clint was watching Heather carefully to make sure that she wasn't trying to bait him somehow. There was always the possibility that she simply knew more than she was letting on and that was also very important.

Heather shrugged and gazed out at the landscape which wasn't much more than a blur of earth tones and smoke from the engine. Before too long, she looked back at Clint and made no attempt to hide the way she slowly let her eyes move over him from his toes all the way up to his hat.

"You don't seem to be wearing a badge," she pointed out. "But you do wear that gun like someone who knows how to use it. I guess I figured that must make you a gunfighter." The smile on her face faded, but the spark in her eyes flared up a bit when she asked, "Am I mistaken?"

"Depends on who you ask," Clint said.

"I'm asking you."

"I could be wearing a badge. You might just not be able to see it."

Heather turned so that she was facing Clint straight on. She took another half-step toward him and let the motion of the train tip her over so that she bumped against him. The moment their bodies connected, she placed both hands on his stomach and slid them over his torso.

"I guess," she said while sliding one hand over his chest and the other down his side, "that all depends on where I intend to look for it."

NINETEEN

The door to Heather's private compartment came open and was immediately forced against the wall by the two bodies who were pressing up against it. It banged against the wall loudly as Clint and Heather all but tumbled into the cramped quarters.

The compartment wasn't much more than a large, glorified closet complete with a narrow bed and two chairs. A table folded out from the wall beneath the window and was held in place by two straps of leather. Neither Clint nor Heather seemed to notice the confined spaces since they were already too involved with each other.

They explored each other's bodies with quick, groping hands. Their mouths pressed together in a kiss that was both hungry and desperate at the same time. Every so often, Clint would feel the touch of her tongue against his lips. When he moved down to nibble along the side of her neck, he felt Heather's arms wrap around him as a lustful sigh came from the back of her throat.

One of Heather's hands left Clint's body for a moment just so she could reach out and make sure the latch on the door was in place. Once she knew the door was locked, she

backed up from Clint so he could see her as she started to
unbutton her dress.

Clint still had his hands on her hips. Even if he could
have backed up any farther, he wouldn't have wanted to.
Holding her there was far too enjoyable, especially as her
body wriggled slightly while she eased the dress down
over it.

The top part of it came down first, exposing the upper
portion of her breasts and then the thin bodice that was on
underneath it. He lifted his hands just long enough for her
to slide the bunched up material down over her hips so it
could finally drop in a pile upon the floor.

When she kicked the dress away, Heather looked up at
Clint with a hungry smile. Her breathing was getting faster,
which was plain enough to see by the way her chest rose
and fell beneath what little material was still covering her.

For a moment, Clint let his eyes wander down her body.
He drank in the sight of her smooth, pale skin. His hands
loosened the bodice that was still wrapped around her until
it too fell onto the floor. His hands quickly found her
breasts and cupped them as soon as they were free from the
constricting material. They were soft and firm, with pink
nipples that were the size of pennies.

He only had to brush his thumbs over them a few times
before her nipples stood erect and Heather was breathing
even harder. Keeping one hand where it was, he allowed
the other to slide down her side, over her hip and down to
her thigh.

"That's nice," Heather purred.

Her hands were busy as well, unbuttoning buttons and
unfastening buckles until Clint's clothing started to fall on
top of her own. His gun dropped heavily to the floor, soon to
be followed by the sound of both of their bodies dropping
onto the narrow bed which took up half of the compartment.

Supporting himself with one knee against the bed's
frame, Clint hovered over her while he brushed his fingers

over Heather's bare skin and stopped for a moment when he got to the region just below her waist. She peeled back the final layer of material, exposing a soft, downy patch of hair that was the same golden hue as the hair the flowed over her shoulders.

Heather started to say something, but the words caught in her throat when Clint's fingers slipped between her legs and started rubbing along the moist lips there. Instead of words, soft moans came out of her as she leaned back and spread her legs for him so his fingers could reach every part of her.

Clint watched as every part of Heather's body responded to his touch. Her nipples stood out even more and her back arched with pleasure. With her head leaning back against the wall, both hands reached out to take hold of him. When he slid a finger inside of her, Clint heard her start to moan his name. One of her legs snaked around him, drawing him closer while the other extended along the edge of the bed.

Suddenly, she took hold of the hand that was giving her so much pleasure. Heather wrapped her fingers around the wrist and gently moved that hand up her body and between her breasts.

Clint let himself be guided by that and started moving up onto her as well. Her legs opened to accommodate him as she pulled his hand up even higher. He was so hard that all it took was a few shifts of their hips before he felt his cock pressing into the welcoming embrace of the lips between her thighs.

Still holding on to Clint's hand, Heather opened her mouth and placed Clint's finger inside just as he was pushing his hips forward to bury his cock inside of her. She was still moaning as she tasted the wetness on his finger while taking every inch of him inside.

The feel of her mouth wrapped around his finger combined with the feel of her pussy wrapped around his cock was enough to make Clint a little dizzy. His own breaths were coming harder now and he reflexively started pumping into her with growing force.

Beneath them, the bed creaked and knocked against the wall. That sound mixed in with the rattle of wheels against track and the general shifting of the entire train around them. It didn't take much for them to find a rhythm that matched that of the train. Once they were there, it seemed that the entire locomotive was rocking to the pace of Clint's hips thrusting between Heather's legs.

Heather wrapped her arms around Clint to steady herself as she pumped her hips in time to his own. She was grinding against his rigid penis until she found the one spot that made her groans even louder. Once there, she clenched her eyes shut and rode him until an orgasm started to spark inside of her like a fire that was being stoked.

As much as he liked being right where he was at, Clint felt himself starting to slip. Between the narrow bed and the rocking train car, he was about a few seconds away from taking a very embarrassing fall. Heather must have sensed it, because she opened her eyes to look at him when he started easing up on her.

Without saying a word, Clint stood up and urged her to do the same. She followed his lead and went where his hands directed her. In no time at all, she found herself turned with her back to him and her knees on the edge of the bed. She didn't need to be guided anymore and leaned down and forward to press both hands against the wall as Clint eased in behind her.

Heather's back was a perfect arch that started at the base of her neck and flowed all the way down to the perfect upward curve of her tight backside. Placing one hand on her firm buttocks, Clint used the other to guide himself once again between the wet lips of her pussy.

If Heather thought he'd found the best spot on her body before, she was immediately proven wrong now. Clint's rigid penis slid easily inside of her and drove in even deeper than before. Both hands were on her buttocks now, guiding both of their bodies into a whole new rhythm.

Heather arched her back and tossed her blond hair over her shoulders, gritting her teeth as a powerful orgasm swept through her entire body. She could feel Clint pounding into her harder and harder. She urged him on by bucking up against him and letting out a groan that came from the back of her throat.

Clint could feel her tightening around him and could see her muscles straining toward another climax. Her skin felt like damp silk beneath his hands and just a few more thrusts were enough to send him over the edge.

Outside, the train whistle blew and the wheels continued to clatter against the rails.

TWENTY

The men chained to their seats were getting restless.

This much was plain to see for everyone inside the compartment. The two Marshals could see the way Trask shifted in his seat, started to speak, thought better of it and then shifted some more. He glared around at the men guarding him as though he meant to snap at them like some kind of animal on a leash.

Redwater's actions weren't quite so obvious. Since he rarely made any movements or said anything at all, the fact that he was starting to squirm a bit was like a flag being dropped. The Indian would occasionally look over to Trask and keep his eyes focused on him until Trask would shake his head or shrug.

Every time Redwater glanced over at him, Trask seemed to get more and more uncomfortable.

Ike stood at his post at the front of the car, standing in the same way as he would when watching over a maximum security prison. From his point of view, the prisoners' thoughts might as well have been written across their foreheads. He kept his own face cold and impassive, however. Doing anything else would have been plain stupid.

"Hey," Trask said. When he didn't get a response right

away, he fixed his eyes upon the closest Marshal and started rattling the chains from his wrists.

Marshal Kelso let out an aggravated breath and turned to look in Trask's direction. "You make any more noise and I'll be forced to chain you down tighter."

"Ain't we got rights to be treated better than that?"

"You should be thankful that your rights have been carried this far, asshole. Now what the hell is bothering you?"

"I thought you said there was shooting."

"Never mind about that."

"Was there shooting or wasn't there?" Trask asked. "If there's trouble, maybe we should be moved to another car."

"There wasn't any trouble."

"I thought I heard someone hollering not too long ago."

"I told you already," Rivera said. "Something just got knocked over. Now shut up."

"I have to piss."

It wasn't so much the question that caught everyone's attention, but the simple fact that it had come from Redwater. So far, the lawmen hadn't heard the Indian say more than two words throughout the entire trip. Now, the sound of his voice was something akin to a low rumble of thunder coming from a cloudless sky.

"You trying to make trouble too?" Kelso asked.

Redwater's eyes shifted in his skull so slowly that they seemed to be scraping along the inside of their sockets. When they fixed upon the Marshal, they stayed there, unblinking.

"No," Redwater said. "I just need to piss."

Kelso studied the Indian for a moment or two, but he would have had better luck trying to study the thoughts going on inside a mountain. If there were any to be known, he was an awfully long ways from knowing them. Kelso decided to just go by whatever information he could gather on his own.

"All right then," Kelso said. "Ike, take this man to the water closet. He's been cooperative enough to earn a walk."

"What about me?" Trask asked. "I been cooperative."

"You've been a wart on society's ass since the day you were born and you've been a pain in mine since I had to take custody of you. I'd suggest you keep quiet before I decide to make you eat the butt of this shotgun."

Trask leaned forward as though he was being lowered by a string. His jaw slacked open and a noisy breath seeped out from between his lips. "What if I gotta piss too, Marshal?"

"Hold it."

"That could get a might messy."

"Make a mess and you'll be cleaning it with your tongue."

Plenty of words sprang to Trask's mind in response to the Marshal's comment. When he got a good look at Kelso's eyes, however, he thought better of it and sucked his words back down again. Like a scolded child, Trask flopped back against the wall and stared straight ahead.

Kelso leveled his shotgun at Redwater and said, "Take the chains off from that post, Ike. If he makes a move, just try to give me a clear shot."

Ike wasn't at all surprised that the Marshal had given him the duty of getting close enough to Redwater to unchain the Indian from the post that held him in place. The Marshals might have told him that he was a valuable member of the team, but Ike also just happened to get all the worst jobs that rolled around.

Rather than bitch about it, Ike stepped forward and did as he was told. The Indian did seem to ease back when he saw who was coming toward him and didn't put up the least amount of resistance. Once the chains were in Ike's hand rather than looped around the post, Redwater perched himself at the edge of his seat and waited.

"Stand up," Ike said once he'd stepped back far enough to take the slack out of the chain.

His shotgun was handed back to him and then Ike

stepped out of the compartment to take a quick look in either direction. Just then, the door at the far end of the car swung open. Ike pivoted to aim in that direction, but relaxed when he saw Clint peeking inside.

Ike gave him a quick nod to let Clint know that everything was all right.

Although he got the message just fine, Clint saw the chain in Ike's hand and knew that there probably wasn't just a pet on the other end of it. For a moment, all the light from inside the compartment was blotted out as Redwater shuffled through the narrow doorway.

Clint stepped outside the car once again and pulled the door shut. When he peeked back through the window, he saw the Indian following Ike toward the opposite end of the car. When nobody else came out to cover Ike's back, Clint decided to take that responsibility on himself.

TWENTY-ONE

The Indian moved as though his feet weren't only chained together, but nailed to the floor as well. He never picked the soles of his feet off the floor and never took a step that was more than a few inches long. Even so, he seemed to be punishing the floorboards with his weight alone and his eyes were like two burning embers.

Perhaps because Redwater rarely even spoke or turned his head, Ike was more willing to let him move at his own speed. After all, he wouldn't fault a statue for being slow if it decided to get up and take a walk. Of course, Redwater didn't look like he would respond to being hurried anyhow.

Ike was sure to keep his distance from the Indian and his shotgun out of Redwater's reach. This was a time when he seemed to be tied to the chain just as much as the prisoner was. Although there were no locks binding Ike's hands or feet, he couldn't exactly let go of the chain either.

The water closet was a narrow room toward the end of the car. It pretty much lived up to its name since it was just a little room with a single seat that opened up to the tracks below. When the Indian stepped into the cramped space, he filled almost every inch of it.

Under normal circumstances, Ike might have broken out

laughing at such a sight. These, however, were anything but normal circumstances.

"You going to close the door?" Redwater asked.

Ike met the Indian's gaze and said, "Just turn around and do your business. Don't worry about me."

Redwater turned his back to the guard and started tugging at the waist of his pants. Without turning around, he asked, "Could I at least move the door shut? I don't think I can fit through this hole in the floor."

"Do what you like. Just know that if I don't like what I see, I'll blast you into small enough pieces so you *can* fit through that hole."

Redwater nodded and reached back with one foot. He caught the bottom of the door with his heel and eased it shut a bit. The door made it less than halfway closed before it was stopped by the chain leading out and into Ike's hand. The Indian seemed content enough with that and got down to the business that had brought him into that little room.

Ike waited outside, listening to every rattle and knock that happened inside the car or out of it. His hand was steady upon the shotgun and didn't let the barrel waver once from the spot Ike had chosen upon Redwater's back.

Ike had been guarding prisoners for enough years to know better than to take his eyes off of one for a second. Plenty could happen in the blink of an eye. The trick was just to make sure that none of it happened to the wrong people.

Before too long, Ike could hear that the Indian was through with his business. The door, however, wasn't coming open just yet.

"All right in there," Ike said. "Get everything where it belongs and get out here."

He could see most of the Indian's back through the crack in the door. So far, Redwater hadn't done much more than shift a little from side to side. Using the barrel of the shotgun, he started knocking on the door's frame.

"I said come out, Redwater."

Inside, the Indian turned, paused, and then turned some more until he was able to open the door and take a step outside.

Ike had his eye on the Indian the entire time. Just as he was about to back up a step to give the prisoner some room, Redwater exploded into a motion that was so sudden it seemed to have come while Ike's eyes were closed during a blink.

The Indian reached out with one hand to grab hold of the shotgun and twist it out of Ike's hand. Although the trigger guard and handle locked his wrist and fingers into a painful position, Ike kept hold of the weapon. It was a simple, yet agonizing, act of survival.

Ike's lips curled back in a silent grimace as his fingers were quickly pushed to the breaking point. His eyes were wide open even though his vision was starting to cloud on the edges from a mix of pain and the sudden rush of adrenaline.

Redwater was closing in on him like a bad dream. His face drawing closer as he used the shotgun to pull Ike in just a little closer. What Ike couldn't see was that Redwater's other hand was reaching for something that had been blocked by the partially closed door.

Struggling against the Indian's incredible strength as well as the pain that was flooding through his system, Ike forced himself to breathe and see past the panic that was threatening to overtake him. What he saw was a barely noticeable curl at the edges of Redwater's mouth.

A smile like that from a man like Redwater meant that Ike had stumbled into a world of trouble.

TWENTY-TWO

The next couple of seconds dragged by on lead feet.

Ike couldn't tell whether Redwater was still trying to get the shotgun from him or was just trying to torture him. So far, the Indian hadn't moved more than a little here and there since he'd sprung forward to make his play.

As much as Ike struggled against him, he simply couldn't get anything to budge. The shotgun wouldn't move within Redwater's fist and when he tried to pull the trigger, he felt the gun twist a bit more instead. The bones in Ike's hands ground together, making a noise like sandstone scraping against slate in his ears.

The joints strained to their limits and Ike could no longer hold back the look of agony.

Ike's brain screamed at him to move, but he couldn't pry away his attention from the struggle for control of the shotgun. It took all of his concentration to just keep the weapon against the wall. If he loosened his grip in the slightest, the gun would belong to Redwater and the trouble would grow by tenfold.

With the blood rushing through his veins, Ike couldn't hear much more than what was going on inside of himself. The sound of the door at the other end of the car reached him, but not by much. All Ike could make out was the faint rumble which carried through the floorboards.

He did see Redwater's eyes shift in that direction, however, which immediately caught Ike's attention. Reflexively, he looked that way also and saw half of a figure standing in the doorway leading from the car, outlined against the incoming sunlight.

"Let him go," came a voice from that doorway.

Redwater glanced over to Ike as if he meant to size up what the guard had left. By the time he was able to look back again, the figure from the doorway was already charging straight for him like he'd been shot from a cannon.

Ike could feel the approaching steps through the already rattling boards under his feet. Sensing that the Indian was distracted for the moment allowed him to focus his thoughts a little more clearly and draw on what little reserve strength he had left. Summoning up just enough wind to fill his lungs, Ike shifted his weight and brought his back leg forward in a powerful forward swing.

The guard's shin caught Redwater squarely in the groin just as the new arrival got close enough to reach out and take hold of the shotgun.

The fire in Redwater's eyes flared up as he turned to get a look at the man who was trying to take away his best chance at freedom. Before the Indian's eyes could get to their target, the other man's fist snapped forward to slam straight into his jaw.

Redwater's head snapped back slightly. For a moment, it seemed as though he wasn't even going to feel the effect of the punch he'd taken. In the next heartbeat, however, he let out a grunting breath before toppling back into the water closet.

"Easy, easy!" Ike said as he felt the shotgun twist against his fingers to send another sobering jolt of pain through his whole arm.

Clint looked down at the shotgun he was holding and

then at the Indian he'd just dropped with a punch to the jaw. "Hold on a second," he said. With a flick of his wrist, he managed to shake the Indian's hand off of the shotgun. From there, Clint gently turned the shotgun so Ike's fingers were pointed at a more natural angle. "How's that?"

"Better," Ike said with a breath that seemed to have been pulled up from the bottom of his feet. "Much better."

Clint looked behind him at the rest of the car and saw the nearest compartment door was open and an old woman's head was peeking out. She pulled her head back in again when another door came flying open and Rivera came steaming into the hall with his shotgun held at the ready.

"What's going on here?" Rivera asked the moment he got a look at the scene at the end of the car. When he saw Redwater propped up against the back wall of the water closet, he looked surprised. When he saw Clint standing there next to Ike, he looked doubly so. "Where the hell did you come from?"

"I was watching from just outside," Clint said, pointing toward the door that was still swinging open at the other end of the car.

As he walked toward them, Rivera glanced back and forth between the door and where Clint had wound up. "Jesus Christ. I heard a bit of a scuffle out here, but not nearly enough to think someone had charged all the way down this hall."

"I don't care if he flew down here on wings," Ike said. "I'm just damn glad he made it. Thanks, Adams. I owe you one."

Clint shook the hand he was offered. "Just doing my part. You handled yourself pretty well with all things considered. I didn't even see him make his move."

"Neither did I." Ike looked as though he was about to kick himself almost as hard as he'd kicked Redwater. "Dammit, I can't afford to be that sloppy."

The fact of the matter was that Clint truly hadn't seen the Indian make his move. He hadn't even seen the first hint that the move was coming. That didn't set too well with him. Not at all.

"Looks like he's coming around," Rivera said, nodding toward the Indian who was grunting and starting to reach out for something to steady himself. "Why don't you make yourself scarce, Clint. We can take it from here."

"You sure about that?"

Rivera nodded. "It'd be better all around if you stayed an ace in the hole. You think he saw your face?"

"I doubt it," Clint replied. "I tried to get here fast enough so he wouldn't get a clear look at me. There's no way for me to say for sure, though."

"Well, we'll have to take our chances. I'd say the rest of this trip shouldn't be much of a problem. After all of this, I doubt these two assholes will be able to blink without getting a gun shoved in their faces."

In a few moments, Redwater's eyes were coming open and he was standing up on slightly wobbly legs. The first thing he did was try to get a look at the other man who'd jumped him when he was about to break Ike into pieces.

Ike and Rivera were the only ones in his sight.

TWENTY-THREE

"What happened?" Heather asked as Clint walked back into the compartment where she was resting. "I thought I heard something."

With the sounds of the fight still thundering through his ears and his knuckles still aching from catching Redwater in the jaw, Clint was amazed that the whole train wasn't bristling. As much as he would have liked to take credit for keeping his steps quick and his actions quiet, Clint knew there was more to it than that.

Like most things, however, the fight wasn't much noticed by anyone else. If it didn't concern them directly, most folks were more than willing to let it pass. They had lives to lead and a loud train around them to help in smoothing everything else over.

"It was nothing," Clint said, thankful for the first time that folks could be so wrapped up in their own worlds. "Just a few hotheads in the next car."

Heather looked concerned for a moment, but that moment passed soon enough. "Looks like your hand is swelling. Did you get hurt?"

Looking down at his red knuckles, Clint shrugged. "Just banged them against a door, is all."

Stepping forward, Heather reached out and took hold of his hand so she could lift it to her lips. She placed a gentle kiss on the reddest of the knuckles while looking up into his eyes. "Speaking of hot heads, there seems to be one in this car right here." Using her other hand to start reaching between Clint's legs, she added, "And I'll bet I know right where to look for another one."

As much as he wanted to let her follow through on the promise in her eyes, Clint stepped back and sat down on the bed before she could reach him. "Not just now, Heather. The conductor will be coming around soon checking on tickets."

"All right," she said with a pouting expression. "I guess it wouldn't do to have someone walking in at the wrong moment."

Clint got a good look into Heather's eyes. There was a heat there that had yet to dwindle. Despite what she'd just said, he could tell that the thought of being rudely interrupted wasn't nearly as unwelcome as she was letting on.

Once again, Clint had to force himself to steer his thoughts back to his job. He'd been lucky that his first distraction hadn't proven deadly for Ike. Risking another one would be just plain stupid.

Clint stood up from where he'd been sitting and gathered Heather into his arms. After kissing her deeply for a while, he brushed her hair away from her face with a gentle hand.

"I've still got some business to attend to," he said once she'd caught her breath. "But don't think that means you're rid of me just yet."

"I guess I can let you go for a while. Hopefully we'll see a bit more of each other before we reach Tombstone. And, when I say more," she added while tugging at his belt buckle, "I mean a lot."

"Sounds like a hell of a way to travel." With that, Clint opened the door to the compartment and stepped outside.

He left Heather on the edge of her bed, looking at him in a way that made him want to say to hell with everything else and lock himself in there with her for as long as humanly possible. Hopefully, he truly would get an opportunity to spend some time with her before they reached Tombstone.

And by "some", he meant a lot.

Now that the train was moving along at full speed and the first stop was approaching, the halls were showing a little more activity. Even the folks who'd paid for private compartments had emerged to spend time in the much more sociable dining car.

As folks started getting tired, however, they started to want some time apart from the rest. The ones who were fortunate enough to have a place to go were again seeking refuge there. Luckily enough, Clint hadn't been far off when he'd told Heather about the conductor making his rounds. He could see the uniformed man stepping into the car at that moment, tipping his hat to anyone who looked in his direction.

Clint was out of the car just as the conductor was knocking on the first compartment and informing them of their upcoming stop. When he looked through the window of the next car, Clint was very happy to see it populated only by a few passengers, none of which were armed or in chains.

There was a lot that could be gathered just by looking at the faces of a few people gathered together. Even if someone had them at gunpoint, there was a certain change that came over the way they walked, stood or even breathed. As far as Clint could tell, the people in that car were doing fine and blissfully unaware of the killers in their midst.

Clint opened the door and put a casual smile on his face. Even though he caught sight of a familiar face, the old lady who'd peeked out during the last part of his struggle with Redwater seemed to be doing much better now. She kept

her eyes averted from him, but wasn't about to make a
scene.

Taking his time walking down the hall, Clint ticked off
the moments in his head while making himself appear as
though he was lost or merely bored. He glanced around
and stepped aside to let anyone else walk by, all while
imagining what the conductor was doing in the next car
and how far along he'd walked. Sure enough, within ten
seconds, the door came open and the same man in uniform
stepped through.

He tipped his hat and smiled to the passengers. Then
again, as polite as he was, he didn't seem to realize that
he'd already tipped his hat to Clint less than a few minutes
ago. Not even the first spark of recognition appeared on his
face as he walked toward him.

Clint made like he was headed for the water closet and
allowed the conductor to make his rounds. When the door
to the Marshals' compartment was opened, Clint made
sure to catch the eye of whoever was the one to deal with
the conductor.

As Clint had figured, Ike was the one who had his tickets in hand. When he spotted Clint, he gave the subtle nod
which was the signal that everything was under control.

So far, so good.

Then again, they weren't in Tombstone yet.

TWENTY-FOUR

Normally, train rides seemed to take hardly any time at all. After all, the iron horses were responsible for joining one end of the country to the other. Compared to riding in the saddle, sitting on a train was a blessing. Compared to sitting in a stagecoach, that blessing was even greater.

This time, on the other hand, riding the train felt about as slow as walking. Clint figured this was mostly due to the fact that he was conscious of every single tick of the clock and every single bit of sound or movement around him. Considering that he was spending so much time on a functioning locomotive, that made for a hell of a lot of sound and movement to keep track of.

He'd had his fun with Heather, but it was getting too close to the end of the line for Clint to distract himself that way again. Instead, he'd taken up a spot in the passenger car that was filled with rows of benches and nearly enough bodies to fill every seat on each bench.

The benches were set up so that every two rows were facing each other. Some said that made for a better chance to get to know your neighbors during the course of the ride. Clint wasn't against being friendly, but this was a ride where he had better things to think about.

Not that he could let on about that, however. Rather than let everyone know that there could be a shooting at any second if something went wrong, he had to sit tight and smile while all the people around him went on about their wives, their children, their grandchildren, their land, their jobs, even their pets.

Clint had a few stories cooked up to cover himself if the conversation was ever turned in his direction. Fortunately, that didn't seem like it was going to happen. While that was a good thing in general, Clint couldn't help but wonder just how highly these people thought of themselves if they thought everyone else was so interested in them.

Judging by the conversations he'd listened to over the course of several stops and several miles of track, those people thought their lives all contained the stuff of legend. Before too long, Clint couldn't help but hope Trask or Redwater would stir up something just so the talking would come to a stop.

"What do you think about that, sir?"

Clint was so surprised that someone was actually talking to him that he had to literally shake his head and snap himself out of his self-imposed stupor.

"I . . . I'm sorry," he stammered. "Were you talking to me?"

The old woman might have been a dead ringer for the old lady who'd spotted Clint knocking out Redwater, except for the shorter hair and different clothes. After a while, all of the busybodies on the train started to look alike.

"Yes, I was talking to you," the old woman said as though she couldn't even believe that someone hadn't been listening to her. "I asked what you thought about what I said regarding the current issue in Mexico."

"I guess I must have fallen asleep for a moment."

"Well, it's absolutely preposterous. They won't even allow the shipment of birds I'd ordered from the jungles to be brought up in less than three weeks."

"What?"

The woman recoiled, but not even because of the sharpness of Clint's tone. She actually looked as though she couldn't understand why Clint wasn't as outraged as she was. "My birds! Young man, I've only been talking about the tropical birds I collect and how a new batch of parrots were supposed to be coming in from the jungles."

She let out an exasperated breath and shook her head while glaring at all of the other nearby passengers for support. "You truly weren't listening," she muttered. "How rude."

For a moment, Clint thought he was sleeping and having some kind of bizarre dream. Just when he thought he was going to lose his mind, he spotted another man in a similar predicament sitting across the aisle from him. Apparently, he was stuck in a heated debate over which brand of barbed wire was best for keeping a herd from straying.

Even though that little bit of solidarity between himself and that other poor soul was comforting, it wasn't enough to make Clint want to stay where he was. Seeing that everyone else on the seats next to him were about to pitch in on the old bird collector's behalf, Clint got up and stepped away from the benches.

"Excuse me," he said without even trying to sound cordial, "but I've got some more important matters to attend to."

A few unkind words were muttered before he was out of earshot, but the conversation regarding parrots was back in full swing before Clint had even left the car. Just getting into the fresh air was enough to make Clint feel better. The ever-present rattle of the wheels was more than enough to drown out the old woman's voice.

Getting his mind steered back to his job, Clint actually felt happy to get back to a place where he might have to face down a chained killer. While thinking of that, Clint found himself stepping back into the car where the Marshals were holding Trask and Redwater. Once inside, Clint stopped and let the door shut behind him.

He didn't move past the Marshals' compartment.

He didn't even move from his spot.

Instead, he stood there as if the floor had been marked with an X. When he looked to his left, Clint saw the narrow door leading to the water closet. Without thinking too much about it, he started heading in that direction. Just before he got there, he noticed someone else headed that way with a somewhat desperate look on their face.

Normally, Clint would have stepped aside and let the poor fellow have his relief. This time, he figured, was a little different.

"Sorry," Clint said with a shrug while stepping into the water closet.

Although the other man in the hall nodded that it was all right, he quickly hustled toward the door which led out to the next car.

Due to the smell in the cramped space, Clint hoped that he would find whatever it was that he was meant to find real quickly.

TWENTY-FIVE

Standing inside the water closet was a whole different story than even standing on the other side of its door. It was like being inside of a large crate with a smaller crate nailed to the floor. The top of that smaller crate had an oval hole sawed out of it and, through that hole, he could see the tracks and ground speeding by.

All of the sounds of the train were amplified in there, while also being muffled at the same time. The rush of air and the rattling of the wheels was even more grating on the ears. Every sound that came through the hole or the walls bounced around inside the enclosed space like a ricochet before finally smacking Clint in the face.

That wasn't the only thing smacking Clint in the face. In fact, if he only had to worry about what he could see and hear, the water closet might be somewhat restful compared to the conversations he'd had to bear recently. But those old ladies didn't smell like rotting wood soaked in human waste. Certainly, it wasn't any worse than an outhouse, but the stench wasn't exactly welcoming either. All in all, Clint wanted to get the hell out of there as quickly as he could.

Just before he was about to do that very thing, Clint realized why he'd been drawn there in the first place. Redwa-

ter must have been the one to request going there in order
for Ike to drag him all the way out of their compartment.
Surely the prisoner could have just wanted to stretch his
legs or relieve his bladder, but a man who'd spent years
confined to a cage would have no problem seeing his way
through both types of discomforts.

One thing Clint knew about human nature was that nobody liked to be cooped up. Any prisoner thought about escape and these two prisoners had already gone through a
bit of planning to make their own escape. Who was to say
that arranging for the fake robbery as a distraction was the
only plan in motion?

That wasn't the only thing that brought Clint into the
water closet and kept him inside that stinking box to look it
over. What kept him in there was something he'd heard
about another prisoner who'd managed to pull off a violent
escape. That one also involved a shithouse as well as the
ambush and eventual death of a guard.

The prisoner's name had been William Bonney, also
known as Billy The Kid.

The Kid had been locked up in the Lincoln County
Courthouse and was being watched over by a deputy
named James Bell. Although Billy was able to get on Bell's
good side, he still never lost track of where his own prior-
ities were. All the time he was locked up in that courthouse, Billy must have been thinking about how he meant
to get out.

It was only natural.

Another deputy by the name of Bob Ollinger wasn't
quite so friendly to The Kid as Bell was. The story went
that Bob liked to threaten Billy with a shotgun loaded with
dimes and never got tired of describing just what those
dimes could do when blasted through his gut.

The Kid had listened to all of the threats and put up with
all of Bob's crap. All the while, he and Bell seemed to form
a loose sort of bond. That bond held up when Bob left Bell

in charge while he went to eat or conduct some sort of business of his own outside of the courthouse.

Billy said he needed to go to the outhouse and Bell didn't have any qualms about taking him. Clint imagined that Billy had been talking or joking the whole way, making sure that Bell felt real comfortable and that he had everything well in hand.

The story varies here and there depending on who's telling it, but there's no denying that Billy somehow got his hands on a gun while he was in or near that outhouse. Some say that The Kid overpowered Bell somewhere along the way and got his gun from him.

Others say he got his hands on a gun of his own. Clint had to admit that he bought into that a lot easier. It was more like The Kid to outdraw someone rather than overpower him. All it would have taken was a friend to plant a gun for him and getting into the outhouse wouldn't have been too big of an accomplishment. Billy had plenty of friends.

In the end, it didn't really matter whose story was right or who'd been there to see what happened. Anyone could make or stick to a theory, but the end result was never in question.

Billy got his hands on a gun and, friend or not, he wound up using that gun to kill James Bell. He then took the shotgun that had been Bob Ollinger's pride and joy and used it to make sure Bob's own guts were the ones to see the light of day.

He rode out of town and took his own sweet time in doing it. Billy simply took a nearby horse and strolled out of Lincoln County like he was on his way to a picnic.

That was Billy's style.

Plenty of folks had to have heard the shots and even seen Ollinger meet his end, but they knew where their own allegiances were as well. They watched him go and didn't raise an alarm until it wouldn't do any good.

Now, Clint didn't think that Trask or Redwater were anything like The Kid, but he was certain that they'd pulled together a few friends before winding up in prison. Having Redwater attempt his violent escape while coming out of the shitter struck a chord in Clint's head and it had been bothering him ever since.

It wasn't until he'd gotten inside the water closet that he really even knew why. Looking back on it now with that story about The Kid's escape from the Lincoln County Courthouse in mind, Clint was glad he'd taken a few moments to stop and think it through.

Clint stepped inside and tried to put himself into Redwater's shoes. He closed his eyes and recalled all that he could about what he'd seen when looking in at the water closet through the window at the other end of the car.

Unable to come up with much more than the obvious fact that the Indian was in the stinking room, Clint turned and even moved as though his ankles were chained. His eyes were cast down, which was when he found something that made him stop and smile.

It wasn't much, but the scratches in the wall behind the door were cleaner than most anything else on the wall, which meant they were fresh. More than that, they looked like they were deep and thin enough to have been made by a blade.

TWENTY-SIX

Clint left the water closet and rushed down the hall to the Marshals' compartment. When he got there, he knocked on the door quickly with his knuckles and stepped aside so he wouldn't be plainly visible to anyone in the compartment. As always, it was Ike who was standing at his post with shotgun in hand and he was the one to open the door a crack.

As soon as he saw that Ike had spotted him, Clint gave a shake of his head and motioned for him to step outside. The door closed immediately and Clint walked toward the end of the car.

"Who was that?" Marshal Kelso asked as Ike shut the door.

Before he said a word, Ike gave a subtle signal to let Kelso know that something might be going on and that he meant to check it out.

"Just the conductor," Ike said. "I'll just go see what he wants."

"Do you want Rivera to go with you?"

"Nah. Shouldn't be necessary."

The prisoners watched everything that went on and soaked up every word that was said. Redwater's face was

103

impassive as always and Trask had been keeping his mouth shut for the last hour or so. None of that changed, but that didn't make the lawmen regard them any differently.

Kelso kept his eye on Ike and waited for a return glance before he let the guard step outside by himself. The intensity in his eyes was more than enough to let Ike know that he would need to give a full report when he got back from wherever Clint wanted him to go.

All of this passed between the two men silently and in the blink of an eye. Ike stepped out of the compartment as if he meant to do nothing more than what he'd said he was going to do. Inside, however, every one of his nerves were on end and he was ready to use the shotgun in his hands at a moment's notice.

He spotted Clint right away, standing near the door to the water closet.

"What's going on?" Ike whispered, all the while looking around to see if there was anyone else about.

Once a young couple at the other end stepped out onto the balcony between the two adjoining cars, the hall was clear. Only then did Clint allow himself to respond.

"You need to search that Indian," Clint said.

"We already did when he got back from using the pisser."

"Search him again."

"Why? What's going on?"

Rather than go into all the details and thoughts that had brought Clint to his conclusions, he motioned for Ike to follow him into the small, stinking closet. Ike stopped short of walking through the narrow doorway.

"Just tell me what's going on here."

"I think Redwater might have a knife on him."

Ike's eyes widened and his hands reflexively tightened around the shotgun. "What makes you say that?"

Clint stepped out of the water closet and pushed Ike inside. "Look behind the door."

The door closed shut about halfway, with Ike's body preventing it from going any farther.

"Now look on the wall at just below waist height," Clint said. He waited for Ike to shift around and get a closer look. "See the scratches?"

Ike didn't respond at first. He did, however, lean in a little closer to get a better look at the wall. Having seen something out of the ordinary was the only reason that could get someone with a functioning nose to do such a thing.

"You see them?" Clint asked again.

"Yeah," Ike responded. "I see them. It looks to me like these were just cut in here recently."

"They look pretty deep."

The door swung open and Ike stepped out. "Yeah. Deep enough for them to be made by a knife that was stuck in there and waiting to be picked up. I can't think of too many passengers that would do a thing like that."

"Not unless they were planting them for a friend of theirs to pick up later."

Ike was already out of the smelly room and heading down the hall. "You think one of those robbers planted a knife before they started turning out the luggage car?"

"Could be. Maybe all the rest of it was just to draw attention away from that. They might have thought everyone would relax if they thought they'd already stopped the main escape attempt."

"I'd like to ask them robbers a few more questions, just to be sure."

"Why don't I take care of that," Clint offered. "You just get back and search that Indian for a knife. Search the other one as well, since the knife might have been passed to him somewhere along the line."

"We've been watching them two like hawks," Ike said. "But I've seen far more happen in my years of guarding prisoners. Men tend to get real creative when they got so

much time to sit and plan things out." He and Clint were
outside the Marshals' compartment. Ike stopped and made
sure Clint was standing well away from the door. "You go
and have another word with them robbers and I'll make
sure everything's all right in here."

Clint nodded and stepped away from the door as Ike
opened it and stepped inside. He stayed put for a bit just to
make sure that the guard wasn't walking into a bad situation. If that Indian did get his hands on a knife, he might
have made his move while Clint and Ike were outside talking about it.

Clint's hand drifted toward his Colt and his eyes focused upon the door. There wasn't any noise coming from
the compartment, but that wasn't necessarily an all-clear
signal.

As if picking up on Clint's thoughts, the guard opened
the door one more time, looked out and gave Clint a nod.
That would have to do for now, so Clint turned and left the
car.

TWENTY-SEVEN

Clint rattled the door to the baggage car a few times before stepping inside. After the would-be robbers had been tied up, the Marshals had made sure to let the porters know about the new addition to their collection of cargo and luggage. Therefore, Clint knew that the robbers should still be the only living things inside that car apart from a rat or two.

Of course, only rats on two legs made sounds like the ones he heard when pressing his ear to the door after giving it a shake or two.

Shaking his head, Clint shifted his feet into a sideways stance and braced himself before lifting the latch that had been locked in place to keep the rats inside. With a single, powerful tug, he pulled the door open and moved so that he was filling the doorway.

The sound of thumping steps had reached his ears long before the door came open, so Clint only stayed in the doorway for less than a second. After that brief amount of time, he was stepping into another sideways stance on the opposite side of the door.

Someone came steaming out of the baggage car like he had a steam engine of his own. His head was down and his shoulders were forward, making him into a human battering ram. Of course, the only problem with that was that there wasn't anything for him to ram.

Since Clint had moved out of the way, the oncoming attacker charged right through a bunch of empty space. His feet were going too quickly for him to stop and so he kept right on going past Clint and toward the little iron balcony.

"Oh Jesus," the man sputtered as he tried to bring himself to a stop. "Oh shit, oh hell!"

His eyes were clenched shut and the words just kept pouring out of his mouth. Since his hands were still cuffed behind his back, he wasn't even able to grab onto anything that could help him come to a stop before charging right off the side of the train.

Suddenly, the man realized that he was still on the train. His eyes opened slowly at first and a smile came to him when he saw that he'd been saved from killing himself. When he saw what had saved him, he wasn't quite so happy.

"You son of a bi—" was all the man got out before his savior swatted him across the face with a quick backhand.

Clint couldn't help but laugh at the guy who'd thought his almost suicidal charge was his best shot at freedom. He laughed a little harder when he realized that the man who'd made the charge was the same robber who'd gotten his nose broken earlier that same day.

Holding on to the robber by the cuffs around his wrists, Clint turned the man back toward the luggage car and shoved him forward. The man was still shaky after being swatted on his broken nose and he was blinking his eyes furiously to try and get rid of the tears that were clouding his vision.

"Hurts, doesn't it?" Clint asked. "You know, I would have thought you wouldn't have any fight left in you after getting your nose busted. I've got to admit, you've got some stones. Of course, you sure as hell don't have much luck."

The robber muttered a few obscenities, but couldn't come up with much more than that. He walked where Clint pushed him and allowed himself to drop back down onto the floor next to the others.

By the look of it, Clint figured that the robber must have just gotten on his feet. None of the others were mobile or even free of their ropes. Clint thought that if they'd had more time, one man on his feet could have maneuvered himself around to free one of the others.

Of course, that was assuming that these fellows could think that straight. Considering the men he was dealing with, that was assuming a hell of a lot.

"What about the rest of you?" Clint asked, looking at each of the other robbers in turn. "If anyone else wants to make their big play, now's the time."

The man with the broken nose backed up against a stack of crates and then slid straight down to the floor. He landed with a thump and looked like he couldn't get up again if he'd tried.

The robber who'd been wearing the red bandanna was on his side and about halfway from getting to his feet. Since the door had been opened, he'd been trying to get his feet beneath him with no success. At the moment, he struggled to get back into a sitting position so he could look at Clint and shake his head.

That just left the man with the full beard. Of the three, he was the only one who hadn't made a move of any kind. Of course, his knee was still wrapped in a thick layer of bandages and he seemed to be hanging onto consciousness by a thread.

"No more wild ones in this bunch?" Clint asked. If this had been the first time seeing these men, he might have felt sorry for them. As it was, he thought he was doing good not laughing at them. "Then why don't you boys just relax so I can ask you a few more questions."

"What the hell do you want from us?" the bearded man

asked. "We told you everything we knew the last time you were here."

The man with the bandanna puffed out his chest and grunted, "Yeah! And that was a while ago. We got to eat. We got wounds that need to be doctored. We haven't even been able to—"

"And that brings me right to what I wanted to ask you about," Clint interrupted.

When Clint turned to make sure the door was locked, he slammed it shut ominously. That was mainly so nobody who took a wrong turn while walking about the train would get spooked by what they found. It was also to make sure the robbers weren't able to draw any strength from seeing the outside world so close to their grasp.

The sound of that door closing was all it took to completely drain the men of whatever resolve they'd been able to build up. Clint had never tortured a living soul, and when he saw those pathetic saps deflate like bellows being emptied of air, he almost felt sorry for them.

Almost, but not quite.

TWENTY-EIGHT

Some time later, Clint was able to get back in touch with the Marshals and set up a time for one of them to get away and have a talk with him. Since the train had several stops to go through, none of the lawmen wanted to leave the prisoners right away. In fact, even deciding on a time to have their talk was a problem. Clint could see that everyone in that compartment was on the edges of their seats.

The prisoners seemed to be like coiled springs that were either going to jump forward or snap in two.

The lawmen fed off of that same energy and added plenty of their own steam as well. Just because they were carrying the guns didn't make their ride any smoother. In fact, it seemed quite the opposite. If Clint didn't know any better, he might have thought that the prisoners had already taken control.

All that kept him from walking into that compartment for a closer look was a quick glimpse of Trask's face during one of Clint's walks past.

As always, Redwater had all the depth of a cave painting, but Trask was a different story. On that single walk where Clint was able to look in at just the right time while the door had been swinging shut, he could see the sweat glistening off of Trask's forehead. That, combined with the way the prisoner fidgeted in his seat, told Clint all he needed to know.

Having played poker for so many years enabled Clint to smell nervousness a mile away. It was along the lines of a vulture sniffing out dead meat. Whatever way someone wanted to look at it, the sense had served Clint well more times than he could count. This time, it told him that the prisoners were just as anxious as their captors.

Although things could have been better, having both parties just as nervous meant that neither one of them was winning. For the moment, that would just have to do.

The clatter of the wheels had become as familiar to Clint as the beating of his own heart. That was why he picked up on it immediately when that sound began to slow down and eventually come to a halt. The train was pulling into a station, marking off one more stop before the line ended outside of Tombstone.

"There you are," came a familiar voice from just behind the spot where Clint was standing.

Clint put on a convincing smile and turned around. When he saw the way Heather looked at him as she drew up closer, that smile became much easier to maintain.

"Just out for some fresh air."

"I don't blame you. Between the smell of all the people packed into that train and the smoke that comes in through the windows, fresh air is pretty hard to come by." She rubbed a hand on his back and looked out at the scenery. "We'll be getting close to Tombstone soon."

"Yep. Where will you be going from there?"

Heather glanced over at him and put on a stern expression. "You're not the only one with business to attend to, you know."

"Fair enough," Clint said with a shrug.

Wrapping her arms around him, she leaned against Clint and rested her chin upon his shoulder. When she whispered to him, he could feel the heat of her breath against his neck as well as the reaction that caused from the rest of his body.

"Let's not worry about any of that," she said softly. "Let's just hope that we meet up again sooner rather than later."

"I'm sure we could arrange something."

"Maybe. But right now, it looks like you've got some business of your own. See you later, Clint Adams."

Brushing her lips against his skin, Heather nibbled on Clint's ear and flicked her tongue against the lobe just enough to send a shiver down his spine. From there, she moved back and walked toward the door leading to the next car.

Before her footsteps faded, they were replaced by the impact of heavier boots against the iron balcony. Clint turned to glance over his shoulder and saw a familiar face looking in his direction. By now, the shotgun in Ike's hand was as familiar as the jacket hanging over his back.

"For someone not trying to draw too much attention," Clint said, "you fellas sure do like carrying those shotguns."

Ike chuckled and stood next to Clint. "It's either that or leave it laying in a compartment occupied by our two esteemed guests. Besides, I doubt there's anyone on this train who doesn't know we're here by now."

"Good point."

As if to indulge Clint for the moment, Ike set the shotgun down and propped it against the side of the train. It took an extra beat for him to actually let go of the weapon, but when he did it was obvious that it was no small relief.

"How's everyone holding up?" Clint asked.

Ike was digging in his front shirt pocket and came up with a cigarette. After placing the cigarette in the corner of his mouth, he fished a match from another pocket and struck it against the railing. "As good as can be expected," he said once the cigarette was burning. "We searched both of 'em right after the last time we talked."

Pausing to dig in yet another pocket, Ike snapped up his hand and flipped a small dagger into view. The blade was less than five inches long and the handle wasn't much more than a nub of wood. "We found this little beauty."

Clint was handed the blade to see it for himself. It was light and sharp as a razor. "Nasty little thing."

"Yep. It's not for whittling, that's for sure. Redwater wasn't too happy when we found it, either. In fact, I think I may have seen the corner of his mouth twitch."

"You find anything else?" Clint asked.

Ike shook his head. "Nope. But that doesn't mean I'm about to let my guard down. Men like those prisoners we got can tell the moment you start to drift off. I'm telling you, I won't get a moment's peace until them two are locked up in their new cells."

Clint felt the same way, but didn't say as much. There was still too much ground to cover on this trail before he could start looking forward to the end.

TWENTY-NINE

The train pulled into a station that wasn't unlike all the others it had pulled into throughout the time Clint had been on board. This one felt very different, however, since this was the station that Clint and the lawmen and even the prisoners themselves had been waiting for.

Over the years, more and more people had been coming to this station since this was the one that was closest to Tombstone. As soon as the iron horse rumbled to a stop and spat out its gout of steam, Clint was waiting to climb down and get his boots onto more steady ground. He was no stranger to riding on a train, but he still preferred the more traditional method of getting from one point to another.

He didn't get a whole lot of time to savor the moment, since there was a whole line of folks behind him waiting to plant their feet on the Arizona soil as well. Stepping aside and walking a few paces down the platform, Clint looked up and down the length of the train.

Down at the baggage car, there were already deputies gathered round to accept the package meant to be delivered into one of their local jails. As arranged by the Marshals, the robbers weren't being taken off the rain until they reached their destination. That way, word wouldn't spread about the possible distraction being removed until it was too late.

There wasn't much of a way for the prisoners to know what was going on inside the train, but they shouldn't have been able to get their hands on a knife either. If anything, keeping the robbers around was worth it just to see the look on Trask's face when he was led down onto the platform as the three men and one dead body were being taken away.

Trask's eyes widened and his lips curled back into a defeated snarl. He even strained at his chains as if he meant to go and finish off the survivors himself. What few words actually made it out of his mouth were just an undistinguishable jumble of profanities.

As for Redwater, the Indian squinted at the robbers and made a short, snuffing sound that passed for a laugh. He then looked to Trask with the words, "I told you so" written all over his face. Not one word had to be spoken.

Passengers streamed out of the train and spread out on the platform to wait for their belongings to be unloaded. Things were held up a bit due to the robbers being carted off, but that only allowed the Marshals and their prisoners to slip away that much easier.

Clint stood facing the luggage car as well, watching Kelso and his men from the corner of his eye. Although he was fairly certain that none of the prisoners had gotten a good look at him, Clint didn't want to take the chance of blowing that now. Redwater got awfully close, but Clint had knocked the Indian down before he'd gotten his eyes too focused on him.

Of course, there was always the possibility that Redwater had seen enough of Clint's face to be able to pick him out again. There was also the possibility that the Indian had even recognized him for who he was. Clint would just have to take that gamble, since he was in this job for the long haul.

He'd already gone through too much to pull up stakes now.

Clint spotted a group of armed lawmen approaching the platform. They were stepping up to meet Marshal Kelso and exchange a few words with him. Clint imagined there was some sort of arrangements to be made regarding the next leg of the ride and didn't bother getting any closer to hear it.

Instead, Clint simply did what anyone else would do after departing their train. He looked toward the luggage car and waited for his own baggage to be dropped out the side of the car. Before too long, Clint spotted his bags and went over to pick them up. By that time, the lawmen and prisoners were walking across the platform and then taking a sharp turn to one side.

The Marshals and their prisoners avoided going through the station and instead walked straight toward a large stagecoach that was waiting to pick them up nearby. Clint had his bags in tow and walked over to stand as close as he could to that edge of the platform without drawing any undue attention to himself. He waited there for a few minutes before one of the lawmen spotted him and found an excuse to break away from the rest of his group.

Rivera walked over to where Clint was waiting and motioned subtly for Clint to follow him as he kept right on going. Once they were out of sight of the stagecoach being loaded, Rivera stopped and let out a haggard breath.

"Just when I think this thing is over, it just keeps right on going," the Marshal said.

Clint nodded. "That was a hell of a train ride."

"Yeah, only you had a much better time than the rest of us, I think."

"What do you mean by that?" Clint asked, eyeing the Marshal suspiciously.

Rivera grinned. "We came looking for you at one point

and walked through the car where you were last spotted. Let's just say it was easy enough to tell that you were in good hands. That blonde that went into the compartment with you must have taken real good care of you."

"If you boys can keep such good track of someone, then why do you need me around?"

Laughing, Rivera patted Clint in the shoulder. "Ike just happened to see you and the lady sneaking off together, that's all. Truth is, I'm glad one of us could have a bit of fun."

"So what's next on the schedule?" Clint asked.

"We're loading them two onto the stage now. That'll take them right out to their cells tomorrow and from there, they probably won't be seeing much of the rest of the world ever again. I still say it would have been a whole lot easier to hang them and be done with it, but I guess this is the next best thing."

"What do you want me to do?"

"Kelso wanted to know if you would be able to meet up with the stage a bit later."

"How much later?"

Shrugging, Rivera took a moment to think it over. "We'll be heading out soon and will stop over in Tombstone. It's not that far of a ride from here, but we'll spend the night in town before moving out to the prison in the morning.

"We'd like to have you meet up with us once we get on the trail. That way, neither of them two will know there's anyone else coming along until it's too late. We're still not certain if anyone else from their gang or such is keeping an eye on them."

"After what happened on the train, I'd say that's a pretty good bet. If I follow up behind the stage, I can check your flanks and make sure you're not being followed."

Rivera nodded. "Sounds great. Marshal Kelso doesn't

say much, but I know he's glad you're coming along for this. He's not the only one, either."

"Thanks. That's good to know."

"I'd better get back. We'll be heading out just after dawn and will be heading southwest."

Clint nodded. "I shouldn't have any trouble keeping up. It's not like you fellas are hard to miss."

Rivera turned and headed back toward the stage. Clint walked in the opposite direction, which took him into the station itself. He was after one thing in particular and found it without too much trouble. Another couple of minutes later, Clint walked out of the telegraph office and saw to renting a seat on a wagon headed into Tombstone.

THIRTY

Between the train ride, the wagon ride and all the work that had gone on in between, Clint felt like he'd been dragged behind a horse all the way from West Texas. He'd been on plenty of longer trails than that one, but not many that had been quite so exhausting.

Some parts of the trip were more exhausting than others and for very different reasons, but tired was tired and Clint was most definitely that. He occupied his mind by thinking back to his time with Heather on board the train and that was almost enough to lull him to sleep. By the time the wagon pulled into Tombstone, the sun was just a silver on the western horizon.

Stepping down from the wagon, Clint tried to think how long it had actually been since he'd left Texas. Thinking all the way back to that point only made him more tired, so he decided to just let it drop. He was in Tombstone now and that was all that really mattered.

The place was alive and well, although not as prosperous as the last time Clint had been there. It wasn't anything against Tombstone itself, but it was a mining town after all and those had a tendency to ebb and flow with their own sort of tide.

While the town wasn't as bustling as he'd last seen it, Clint didn't think for a moment that it was anything more than a slow patch. Despite its name, Tombstone was a living thing that had just fallen on some hard times. It would bounce back surely enough. In fact, as Clint turned and walked down Allen Street, he thought he might be seeing a turn already.

The Occidental boasted entertainment of all sorts and was the host of more than its share of all-night poker games. People flowed in and out of there like a river, spilling out onto the streets and into some of the other nearby saloons. Normally, Clint's first stop would be in one of those saloons. When Wyatt Earp was a resident, he'd owned a stake in The Oriental and Clint would always find himself there whenever he had the chance.

But times had changed since those years. The Earps weren't welcomed in Tombstone as much as they were. Even though the smoke had cleared from the OK Corral, plenty of locals still had the gunshots ringing in their ears and had chosen their sides based on rumor and harsh words more than anything else.

All of this fell onto Clint's shoulders as he walked down Allen Street. By the time he got closer to The Occidental, he felt like a soldier returning to a field that had once played host to a battle. There were no more shots being fired, but the place still smelled like blood and smoke. Of course, the former part of that wasn't exactly true in Tombstone.

"Get the hell outta here, you damn transient!" came a gruff voice from The Occidental.

Just then, the doors to the saloon flew open and a man came backpedaling onto the boardwalk. His arms flailed at his sides to try and maintain his balance, but he failed miserably and dropped flat onto his ass with a grunt.

Even before he tried getting up again, the man reached for a gun that had been wedged under his belt. That was the

moment that the door came open again to allow a man easily twice as big as the first to step through.

"What're you gonna do?" the big man asked without
seeming to care about the gun in the fallen man's grasp.
"You gonna try and shoot me when you're too damn drunk
to walk?"

The man on the ground started to pull the gun from his
belt, but was unable to get it out. Between the barrel getting
snagged on his clothes and his hands too shaky to do much
about it, the fellow wound up pounding his hand against
the ground in frustration and flopping onto his belly so he
could get his legs beneath him.

"That's what I thought, you damn fool," the bigger man
said as he stepped up and hoisted the fallen man up by the
back of his pants. "Come on in here and have a drink on
me. You'll do a whole lot less damage if'n you just pass out
and be done with it."

Clint stood in his spot, watching the scene unfold no
more than twenty yards away from him. He focused his
eyes on the bigger man at first until he realized that there
was no gun on him that he could see. Although that didn't
necessarily mean the big man was unarmed, Clint shifted
his eyes over to the drunk who still had his pistol in plain
sight.

The drunk got to his feet and wobbled there for a moment as his hand dangled toward his gun. At any moment,
he could either pass out or make another grab for the pistol.
He could walk into the saloon and have his free drink or he
could try to end the life of the one who'd helped him up.

Clint decided to stay put and watch to see which of
those things would happen and step in before they took a
turn for the worse.

The drunk got a look on his face that wasn't good. His
lips curled and he tried to say something. His eyes narrowed as he hunkered forward to try and keep his balance.

Clint found his hand drifting toward his Colt in expectation that he might have to do something to keep someone from dying right in front of him.

The drunk sucked in a breath as the bigger man turned his back on him and headed back into the saloon. Seeing that, the drunk straightened up as best he could, raised both hands up to waist level and took a step forward. He landed on one boot and stopped before falling over again. He then lifted his chin and kept his eyes centered on the door to the saloon.

Clint waited.

Pulling in another breath, the drunk leaned back and then forward again as he made his move. His hands came up to his belt, grabbed hold of the worn leather and then clenched as his body crumpled forward and a stream of puke came exploding from his mouth.

"Goddammit!" the big man screamed from inside the saloon. "You'll be the one cleaning that!"

Relieved, the drunk wiped his mouth and stumbled back into the saloon, nearly slipping on his own vomit.

Clint looked around and saw that he was the only one who'd even stopped to take notice of what had just happened.

Chuckling to himself, Clint shook his head and started walking again. "I guess some things don't really change after all," he muttered.

THIRTY-ONE

Clint never made it to The Oriental, The Occidental or any other saloon in Tombstone. In fact, the only place he did make it to was a comfortable bed and a hearty breakfast before the sun had even cracked the horizon. There would be plenty of time for everything else once the work was done.

The first thing on Clint's list was to visit the telegraph office just a bit farther down on Allen Street. When he got there, he found a message already waiting for him. It read:

GOT THE FIRST NOTE **STOP**
IF NEED ASSISTANCE JUST ASK **STOP**
RICK

Clint smirked and had a reply sent back to Hartman. It was short and to the point, letting him know that things were still going well enough and that he should be writing back again within the next few days. If he didn't hear from him by then, that's when he should worry.

When Clint looked out the window, he could see the sky turning the deep shade of purple which meant that daylight would be breaking out in force real soon. The dry desert heat felt good on the air when he pulled it into his lungs. Stepping out onto the boardwalk, he could see why so many men of ill health came out west to live out their years.

Thinking along those lines, Clint couldn't help thinking about one such man who'd walked these very streets not all that long ago. The last time he'd seen Doc Holliday, Clint had wished him the best. Doc hadn't been in the best of health and hadn't gotten any better since then.

Shaking his head, Clint had to admit that he missed the gun toting dentist. Doc was a good man at heart. Then again, that heart was sometimes hard to find beneath everything else that had made him a wanted man in more than one state.

Tombstone was full of memories. All in all, Clint was glad to be putting most of them behind him.

The Marshals were supposed to be loading up their stage again and departing from the end of Fourth Street. Clint walked down in that direction to check in and make sure that everything was going according to the plan. Sure enough, when he got there he caught sight of Marshal Kelso having a word with another lawman. Clint couldn't be certain from where he was standing, but he guessed the other man to be town law.

After finding a good spot in the shade, Clint watched as both Trask and Redwater were escorted onto the stage and locked into their seats. It didn't look as though either of the prisoners were giving anyone any trouble. In fact, they seemed downright sedate compared to the last time they'd been boarded up and locked down.

Although Clint was glad to see everything running smoothly, he couldn't help but wonder if it was just the calm before the storm. The prisoners could just be biding their time, but until when? The stage would head out into the desert where the prison had been built to store problems as nasty as Trask and Redwater. There wasn't much else along the way, which made Tombstone seem like the prime place for one last break for freedom.

Then again, it had been a long haul and two escape attempts had already been thwarted. That left the possibility that the prisoners had already fired off their shots and were grudgingly forced to take what was due to them.

From what Clint had been told about the place Trask and Redwater were headed, it sounded as though the prisoners had pissed off more than a few judges along their way through the courts. Either that, or neither man could hide their murderous natures even though there wasn't enough proof to land them at the end of a noose.

The prison where that stage was headed didn't even have a name. It wasn't even known if there were other prisoners there. It was one of those places where people went to and were never seen again. The only trick was to make sure the right people got there.

Clint started to wonder if he was just getting overly cautious in his advancing years. Then again, if a man like him wouldn't advance too many years more if he started giving everyone else the benefit of the doubt. There was a fine line between being wary and jumpy, just like there was a fine line between being too easygoing and dead.

So far, wariness had never done Clint any harm so he decided to keep right on thinking his gloomy thoughts until Trask and Redwater were in their own private little holes in the middle of the desert. After that, he could relax all he wanted.

THIRTY-TWO

The road beneath the wagon's wheels was rough and well traveled. The ground was like Sheetrock with a fine layer of grit scattered over the top of it and the ruts looked like two trails left by a giant's fingers. As the wagon rolled along those ruts, its wheels rattled within them. Whenever the horses started to pull it an inch or two in the wrong direction, the whole carriage would start to tremble and shimmy.

The wagon itself was a bit larger than a standard passenger carrier. It was about a foot or so wider as well as a couple feet longer. Inside, it was stark and boxlike. Made to carry prisoners instead of passengers, it had two benches that looked more like closed caskets nailed to the floor and a thick wooden pole running from floor to roof at each corner.

Trask and Redwater sat at opposite corners from each other, their arms and legs secured to their own poles. Although they were able to stay on their benches, it was obvious from the moment the stage started moving that comfort hadn't been much of a concern to the builders. The prisoners rattled against the benches and the poles like fresh kills on upended spits.

The Marshals sat with one on each of the benches as
well. This time, rather than shotguns, they each carried rifles to complement the pistols strapped around their waists.
Ike sat facing all four of them on a small seat that wasn't
much more than a square piece of wood that folded out
from the side of the carriage just below the window.

On top and outside the carriage, there was a driver as
well as a man who sat beside him, riding shotgun. The
driver carried a holstered pistol and the man beside him
held a shotgun in both hands with plenty of spare shells in
a leather bandolier over one shoulder and across his chest.

The wagon rumbled along the trail, not moving an inch
when there came another group of horses or smaller stage
bound for Tombstone. If any of the other traveler had anything to say to the wagon when they passed, they kept it to
themselves once they got a look at the armed men riding it.

With the racket of the wagon wheels bouncing along the
rocky ground combined with that of the horses, it was no
wonder that the other rider dogging their trail went unno-
ticed. It was easy enough to miss someone riding on the
same trail until they were almost under the wheels. Spot-
ting someone who didn't want to be seen was a downright
chore.

Clint had given the wagon a two hour head start. Part of
that was to make sure he wasn't riding on the heels of the
wagon where he would be spotted immediately by anyone
staring out the window. Another reason for it was to test the
mettle of the horse that he'd been forced to rent in
Eclipse's absence.

It had been a while since Clint had needed to size up a
horse for himself. Normally, Eclipse was always there for
him no matter what needed to be done. With Eclipse in
Labyrinth and Clint in need of a set of faster legs than his
own, he didn't really have much choice.

When he'd gone to rent a horse, he told the man he

needed it for fast riding over possibly rough terrain. Although the renter had to think for a moment, his daughter didn't pause for a second. She'd gone straight back to a stall and came out with a brown and white Mustang.

"We used to call her Petticoat," the girl said. "On account of her coloring."

Sure enough, the brown patches of the horse's coat were cropped in such a way that made it look like the horse was dressed up in a petticoat. The Mustang tugged at the reins and bobbed her head the way many of the wild breed were known to do. But she took direction well enough and had a certain fire in her eyes.

"Aw, what did you go and get that one for?" the renter said in a scolding tone. "Can't you see Mr. Adams here needs something better than some Mustang?"

"But he said he needed one that was fast and can climb!" the girl shot back. Turning to look at Clint once again, she straightened up and told him, "I said we used to call her Petticoat, but we don't no more. Now we call her Bobcat, on account of the way she runs and charges up into the mountains like they was level ground."

The renter shook his head and added, "Remember something, Mr. Adams. This girl's mountains ain't nothing but some tall hills and a few ridges she found when out riding."

"They was rough terrain!"

Ignoring the bickering pair, Clint was looking the Mustang over a bit closer. She didn't shy away from him but, more importantly, she gave off a certain kind of energy that seemed awfully familiar to him.

"Her legs are strong," Clint said. Nodding toward the young girl, he added, "And I'll take your word about the rest of her. You got yourself a deal."

Just to put a smile on her face, Clint handed over his money to the girl before saddling up the Mustang. She was beaming brightly enough to throw off a spark by the time he rode out of there. As for Bobcat, she had more than lived up to her name.

After putting some distance between himself and Tombstone, Clint snapped the reins to see what the horse had to offer. She responded a bit hesitantly at first, but quickly grew accustomed to her rider and finally gave Clint the speed he'd been asking for.

Mustangs were like that, Clint knew. They had a tendency to pick who they would work for rather than the other way around. Clint had been around enough of the feisty breed to recognize when they'd found someone they could take orders from. Besides that, he'd also seen a bit of Eclipse's wildness in Bobcat's eyes. It was almost as if his good friend was joining him in spirit.

"Come on, girl," Clint said while snapping the reins again. "I know you've got more than this."

As if she took those words for a challenge, Bobcat gave Clint a snort before hunkering down and pouring even more steam into her stride. The Mustang raced over the rocky ground like a bow from an arrow. Every so often Clint would steer her one way or the other just to get a handle on how she took his orders.

Although a bit slow to respond at first, she warmed up well enough. Eventually, all Clint had to do was nudge her with his knee or heel to get her to turn the way he wanted her to go. The trail opened up soon and eventually gave way to more rocks and sand in nearly every direction. Once again, he thought he'd test Bobcat by steering her off the trail.

She took those orders without a moment's hesitation.

Some horses were so accustomed to riding a trail that they hesitated to go off of it. Those were usually horses who'd served out most of their lives in a team or merely acting as transportation. Bobcat was no such animal. She welcomed the chance to go off the beaten trail and even seemed a little hesitant to go back to it.

She charged up a few rises and stopped within a heart-beat after Clint pulled back on the reins. It was almost as though both of them were thinking along the same lines. Either that, or Bobcat knew the lay of the land better than her rider and wasn't about to do anything stupid whether he asked her to or not.

The ride chewed up miles of land and told Clint that the renter's little girl sure knew what she was talking about. Clint had to fight to keep the trail in his sights. It was even a struggle to pull Bobcat around toward it when he figured they were catching up to the stagecoach.

Part of him wanted to just trust the Marshals to their job and their ability to handle two chained men. Clint was having too much fun and, judging by the spirit in Bobcat's galloping strides, he wasn't the only one.

THIRTY-THREE

"You know something? I'm getting real sick of lookin' at that face."

When Trask spoke those words, he did so with an unmistakable snarl. In fact, he seemed to roll each word on his tongue like it was a bug that had crawled into his mouth before spitting it back out again.

His arms dangled from his shoulders since he couldn't lower them all the way with his hands being chained to the post. His legs were also splayed out in front of him with the chain between his ankles also wrapped around the post.

Marshal Kelso leaned back in his seat next to Redwater. His rifle was pressed against the side of the carriage by one leg. His arms were folded across his chest and his head lolled back and forth along with the steady jostling of the wagon.

"That's funny," Kelso said. "I was just about to say the same thing."

"Guess you won't have to put up with it much longer," Trask said.

"Nope. I sure won't."

"That is, until I go to trial again."

Kelso shook his head. The motion could barely be distinguished from the natural motion of his body getting shaken by the bumps of the road beneath the wagon's wheels. "You had your trials. You know that."

Trask smiled and leaned back as much as his chains would allow. "Yeah, I sure did. And they couldn't make nothing stick."

"Three counts of robbery don't sound like nothing to me."

"It is nothing. That is, compared to all the men I killed."

If Trask was looking to get a reaction from the Marshal, he didn't get one. All he did get was another couple of shrugs. This time, there was no way to tell if Kelso was actually moving or if he was just letting himself be rocked by the stagecoach itself.

Next to Trask, Marshal Rivera shifted up to the edge of his seat. He didn't like the way Trask was tensing his muscles while starting to sit up. Rivera's hands clenched around his own rifle, but didn't go so far as to point the weapon or lay a finger on the trigger.

"Shut up, Trask," Rivera said. "You'll have plenty of time to hear yourself talk in your cell."

Trask shot the Marshals a yellowed smile as his eyes darted in between the both of them. As he looked from one lawman to another, he tended not to focus on either one. Instead, he paid more attention to his fellow prisoner by looking at Redwater every time his eyes passed over the Indian.

Redwater hadn't moved more than an inch total since he'd been locked into his seat. Most of that movement was the stage's fault as it jostled everyone inside of it. The Indian looked straight ahead, but seemed to see everything.

After riding with the man for this long, Rivera seemed to be afraid of Redwater. By this point in the trip, that much was apparent to anyone with eyes in their head and the will to pay attention. Marshal Kelso didn't think much of Redwater, but that wasn't exactly the smartest way to go either. The only one with a steady, unwavering view of Redwater was Ike Samuels.

The guard had watched Redwater closely from the first second after taking the Indian into custody. That vigilance had only grown as the trip wore on and tripled after the knife was found tucked away in Redwater's boot.

Ike's eyes narrowed as he picked up on a bit of movement on the Indian's part. It wasn't much and in anyone else, it might have been overlooked. But Redwater was a far cry from anyone else and he made every single move count.

"What's that you're doing?" Ike asked, leaning forward on his seat.

The Indian didn't so much as twitch. His hand froze where it was and the rest of him barely seemed to register any signs of life.

But Ike wasn't about to be pacified so easily. He shifted forward a bit more, stopping just short of bringing his gun to bear. "You heard me, Redwater," Ike said. "Let's see them hands."

The Indian stared straight ahead. There was a difference this time. Redwater's eyes were no longer blank and passive. They were searing with an inner fire like windows looking into a furnace. Almost imperceptivity, the Indian glanced in Trask's direction.

Marshal Kelso was just looking up to take the situation seriously, so he hadn't caught the glance.

Rivera was sitting at a bad angle to see the subtle shift in Redwater's eyes.

Ike, on the other hand, could see it just fine. Rather than let on, he kept his face unreadable and his hands on his weapon. He had a fire of his own boiling behind his eyes and he made sure that the Indian could feel every last bit of it.

Trask was still fidgeting so much that it was hard to tell whether he was hiding something, being tossed about by the stagecoach or was simply having a fit. He looked over to Redwater, but he was also glancing around at everyone else inside the carriage.

Watching that one out of the corner of his eye, Ike decided right away that he wasn't about to see anything useful from Trask. Although he focused in on Redwater even more, he wasn't about to put Trask in his blind spot anytime soon.

Finally, Kelso straightened up and shifted his rifle so that it was laying across his lap and aimed at Redwater. "We know you're not deaf," he said. "Put up those hands."

Redwater's eyes shifted within his skull until he got a good look at the rifle in Kelso's lap. His gaze stayed there as though he and the single black eye of the rifle barrel were having a stare down. The unblinking barrel won, causing Redwater to turn his eyes toward Kelso instead.

Slowly, the Indian lifted his hands and held them in place. The chains swung from his wrists and a couple links scraped against the wooden pole.

The Marshals relaxed a bit and Kelso propped his rifle once again between his leg and the wall of the carriage.

"Good boy," Kelso said sarcastically.

Ike wasn't relaxing. He wasn't even close to relaxing. He might have eased his back up against the wall, but his hand was still tight around his weapon. Every muscle in his body was showing the wear and tear of the whole trip, but he wasn't about to give in to the strain. He knew the prisoners had something else up their sleeves.

It was only a matter of what it was and when it would be dropped.

THIRTY-FOUR

Clint had been to Tombstone enough times to know the terrain fairly well. He'd approached the town from practically every direction, which was how he figured the stagecoach's route without having to catch sight of it once. More than that, he'd already figured the best way to not only catch up with the stage, but flank it from higher ground.

So far, the rented Mustang was performing like a champ. Clint figured that Bobcat must have truly taken a shine to him, or that the renter didn't know a good horse from a hole in the ground. Whichever it was, Clint didn't much care. All he did care about was getting within sight of the stage before too much of the day had burned away.

They made it to a perfect spot in less time than even Clint had imagined.

When she got to the base of the rise, Bobcat paused for a second before lowering her head and charging in the direction she was steered. That showed that she'd either picked the same way herself or that she was starting to trust Clint even more. Knowing Mustangs, the former was a whole lot likelier than the latter. Whichever it turned out to be, all Clint needed to do was hold on and enjoy the ride.

The trail was narrow and twisted. Actually, it was more

of a barely visible footpath than a trail, but it served its function well enough and led all the way to the top. As it turned out, the rise was a rocky slope of loose gravel and small boulders on one side and a sharp drop-off on the other. After navigating the loose gravel and boulders, Clint found himself looking down on the trail as it turned sharply and snaked off into the distance.

Clint lowered himself from the saddle and moved over to Bobcat's side so he could get to his saddlebags. It was still odd to have a horse other than Eclipse for the ride, but he knew he'd be back with the Darley Arabian stallion soon enough.

Bobcat fussed and shifted as Clint tried to get around her. She stomped every so often and shook her head as if she wanted to run some more with or without Clint in the saddle. Even when Clint took hold of the reins and tried to calm her down, Bobcat kept fidgeting until she finally ran out of steam.

"Easy now, girl," Clint said as he patted the Mustang's neck with one hand while fishing in the saddlebag with the other. "We'll be off and running soon enough."

Although Clint found what he was looking for, he was beginning to see why the horse renter had rolled his eyes when he'd gotten a look at what his daughter was bringing to one of his customers. Someone who didn't know their way around the animal would have a hell of a time with Bobcat.

In fact, Clint had yet to see if he wasn't going to run into a bit of hell farther down the road.

For the time being, Clint was glad to have covered so much ground. After pulling a spyglass from the saddlebag, he crouched down and made his way to the edge of the rise. His instinct was to let the reins go so he didn't skyline the horse as well as himself. With Bobcat, however, Clint didn't think he could allow so much slack.

It took a few moments, but he led the horse to a spot beneath the edge of the rise that had a few sprouts of grass poking up to keep the horse busy. That spot was at the limit of the reins' length, but Clint was able to keep the leather straps in hand while he got himself situated on the rise one more time.

The spyglass came open with a flick of the wrist and Clint lifted the smaller lens to his eye. He found a spot close by and followed it out, but was more interested in a bunch of dust that was being kicked up in the distance.

He found the dust without any problem and kept the spyglass pointed in that direction until enough of it cleared for him to see through it. Sure enough, the Marshals' stage-coach was the source of the dustup. Clint could spot the big wagon easily enough. There weren't too many stages that size crossing the country. If he needed any more confirmation, the two armed men in the driver's seat were a pretty good giveaway.

Just to be certain, Clint kept his lenses pointed at the wagon itself. He wanted to see at least one more sign that he'd found the right wagon. The biggest mistake he could make right now was tailing some traders or a payroll delivery instead of the ones who truly needed his help.

As if on cue, the dust parted and Clint got a clear look into one of the windows. The first face he could see was Ike's. His black skin stood out from a distance compared to all the dust and backs of heads that Clint could make out. Although it wasn't a face, Clint could also see the unmoving statue that was John Redwater. That Indian filled up space like a storm cloud and had the presence to match.

"All right," Clint said to himself as he folded up the spy-glass and shimmied down the ridge. "Looks like they're still on course."

The reins had slipped from Clint's hand and Bobcat seemed to sense it even before the leather hit the ground. The Mustang let out a huffing whinny from the back of her throat and started to step sideways away from Clint.

"No time for this, Bobcat," Clint said as he walked a bit quicker toward her. "We've got to go."

But Bobcat gave him nothing more than half a glance before shaking her head and easing herself a few more steps away.

Clint stopped where he was and kept still. He was no expert in breaking wild horses, but his instincts were good enough to tell him when one was thinking of taking off on her own. Rather than make any sudden moves, he kept eye contact with Bobcat and stepped forward slowly. He lifted his feet just high enough to keep from scraping on the ground, but kept them low enough so his steps weren't obvious.

Bobcat shifted a bit, but let Clint get a little closer. With a single, lightning quick motion, Clint snapped his hand out and took hold of the reins. Defeated, Bobcat didn't give him any more trouble as he saddled up.

"Come on, girl. Let's see if a little more running will settle you a bit."

THIRTY-FIVE

Trask shifted in his seat, grunting and clearing his throat as if the sound of the wagon's wheels weren't enough to fill everyone's ears. Every so often, he would try to cover his mouth or scratch behind his ear. And every time he did any of those things, his hand would pull the chain taut to make yet another sound to rattle everyone inside the wagon.

"For Christ's sake, will you knock that shit off?" Marshal Kelso snarled.

At the moment, Kelso was sitting across from Trask and Rivera was sitting across from Redwater. Although the Marshals changed their positions every so often, Ike stayed right where he was. That was his own choice, however, since he preferred to watch over them in a way he was more accustomed to.

Kelso leaned forward a bit. The motion caused his leg to push the rifle up against the wall with a solid thump. Rather than say anything, he leveled an intense glare at the prisoner until Trask finally slumped back into his seat.

Nodding, Kelso leaned back as well. "That's better," he said.

Rivera sat with his head leaning back as if he was about to doze off. He'd been tense at first with the constant friction between Trask and the others, but after a while even that distraction had worn off. Rivera made it his job to keep his eye on Redwater, but the Indian wasn't doing anything but sitting and staring straight ahead. Even though his face was pointed at Rivera, Redwater somehow managed to not look at him.

The shaking of the stagecoach was too irregular for anyone to fully become accustomed to it. Still, it was wearing off on the men as well. It took a sudden thump of the wheels finding a hole in the road followed by the entire wagon jumping to catch Rivera's attention now.

After nearly smacking his head against the roof of the stage, Rivera grabbed hold of his guns to make sure they didn't fall too close to any of the prisoners. He kept the weapons nearby, but when his head snapped downward after he landed back on his seat, Rivera spotted something else.

"Hey," the Spaniard said while staring at one of Redwater's ankles. "What happened to you?"

The Indian ignored him at first, but then started to look down when he saw that Rivera wasn't about to let him be. "I'm fine," Redwater grunted.

But Rivera wasn't pacified by that. Instead, he leaned in a bit to get a closer look. He stopped well out of the Indian's kicking range and when he looked up, Marshal Kelso was looking over at him.

"What is it?" Kelso asked. "What're you talking about?"

"His ankle," Rivera said, nodding toward the Indian's leg. "Looks like he's hurt."

Ike shifted so he was facing the Indian a little better, but made sure to keep his back pressed firmly against the wall. His hands also closed around his weapon as the hackles started to raise along the back of his neck.

Redwater was wearing dark denim pants and old, battered leather boots. Because of that, it had been easy enough to miss the way the cuff of his left leg had become a bit darker than the rest of the material. Only through a stroke of luck and some sharp eyes would someone truly pick out the subtle glistening of that cuff until it had been thoroughly soaked.

Ike looked up at Redwater's face, but knew better than to expect anything else but his impassive mask. "You hurt?"

Redwater shrugged. "Must have cut myself when I got onto the stage. These chains are biting into me. Could be them too."

Suddenly, Trask started flailing at his chains and kicking his feet as though he was throwing a fit. "You see what I been telling ya?" the prisoner shouted. "These cuffs need to be loosened. We ain't animals, you know! We should be treated like human bein's!"

Kelso wheeled around to face Trask and this time, he brought up his rifle to aim at the prisoner. "You shut yer goddamn hole, Trask! I am sick to death of you!"

Rivera glanced over toward Trask and Kelso, but Ike kept his eyes fixed upon Redwater. That was why he was the only man to see the Indian's hand flash down toward his bloody pants cuff while lifting his leg to meet it. Redwater pulled the material up to expose a shin that was so bloody, it seemed to have discolored the very hue of his skin.

A gash had been cut into his flesh that was so deep, the meat there was separated enough to hold on to a second knife and keep it in place. Ike watched the whole thing as though it was moving in half-time. He screamed inside to get himself to move and his body was already responding.

In the back of his head, however, the guard feared that it was already too late to do anything more than watch.

THIRTY-SIX

Redwater reached down to grab the nub of a handle protruding from his leg so he could pull it out.

The knife came out amid a spray of blood while Redwater's free hand reached out to grab hold of Marshal Kelso by his shoulder. Redwater pulled the lawman close enough so his other hand could bury the knife into the Marshal's gut.

Kelso let out a grunt that was more surprised than pained. His eyes widened into saucers and his mouth opened into a gaping expression as a breath seeped out from deep inside of him. Just as he was about to try and pull in a breath to fill his lungs again, Kelso felt the Indian's grip on him tighten as the knife was pushed up into him even more.

Rivera acted as quickly as he could, but found himself fumbling to get his weapon up and ready to fire. Before he could even put a finger against his trigger, Trask's hands lunged out for him and got hold of his right sleeve.

"No, no, no you don't," Trask hissed.

In fact, Trask had only been able to get a one-handed grip on the Marshal. He was able to pull Rivera with enough force that the lawman was taken off balance so he started to lean toward Trask. The motion of the stagecoach

143

took care of the rest and delivered Rivera straight into Trask's clutches.

As this was going on, Ike was anything but a mere spectator. The guard's reflexes had been quick, but he was knowledgeable enough to know that he wouldn't be quick enough. That didn't keep him from acting as he gave up on his rifle and instead went for the pistol at his side.

Ike's change of plan didn't cost him a bit of time as each hand worked on their own without hindering the other. Even so, by the time he cleared leather and felt his finger slide through the trigger guard, he saw that Redwater was moving just as quickly despite the chains he wore.

The Indian moved so quickly that the irons around his wrists barely scraped against the pole secured within the coach. Rather than worry about the Marshal who was still struggling to get control of himself and his weapon, Redwater shifted his eyes over to Ike while he pulled Marshal Kelso across the front of his body.

Still groaning and struggling to keep his head up, Kelso found himself off his feet with the knife still held firmly in his stomach. On reflex, he reached up to try and pull the blade out of him, but Redwater's hand was still gripping it tightly. He tried to struggle and get away from the Indian, but he couldn't even figure out exactly what was happening. The world was teetering too far away from his senses and the pain was threatening to put him out completely.

While Kelso did his best to put up a fight, Redwater had picked him up and was handling him like a rag doll. Keeping the knife in place without driving it in too far, he swung the Marshal around until he had Kelso in front of him as a human shield.

Ike had the rifle up and was ready to fire. The only problem was that he was now aiming at the pale face of Marshal Kelso rather than Redwater's familiar stony visage.

"Put him down!" Ike shouted.

Redwater peeked over Kelso's shoulder like a demon.

Strangely enough, there was still hardly a flicker of emotion registering in his eyes even as he slowly caused the life to seep out of Kelso's body.

With this going on, the other side of the stagecoach felt as if it was a hundred miles away. On that side, Trask and Rivera still struggled amongst themselves with one man trying to get his hands on a gun while the other fought like hell to prevent it.

Rivera started to look and see what was going on between Redwater and the other lawmen, but was pulled back into his own fight as Trask snapped his knee up and knocked it straight into the Spaniard's jaw. Trask followed up with an elbow that came crashing down upon Rivera's shoulder among the metallic jangle of the chains dangling from his wrists.

"I said put him down!" Ike repeated. "Now!"

But Redwater didn't say one word in reply. Instead, he shook his head just enough for Ike to see it and lifted Kelso up a bit higher. Under other circumstances, the sight of the big Indian carrying Kelso like that might have been comical.

It stopped being funny when Redwater started slowly twisting the knife in Kelso's belly and tightening his grip when the Marshal started to kick and squirm.

In all his years of dealing with dangerous men in terrible places, Ike had never gotten into a spot where he didn't have a notion of what to do.

That is, he hadn't gotten in a spot like that until now.

THIRTY-SEVEN

Clint sat hunkered down in the saddle with his upper body leaning forward against Bobcat's back. He could feel the horse racing beneath him. In fact, it felt more like he'd managed to rope a twister and was somehow able to hang on.

Eclipse was known to take him faster than he'd expected and even thought possible sometimes, but this Mustang was something else entirely. With Bobcat, Clint could feel the animal's wildness so close to the surface that he wondered who'd been able to get a saddle on her at all. That feeling only grew more powerful as Clint let the Mustang run flat out over the Arizona ground.

It had taken a while to get back onto Bobcat's good side again. Once he was there, however, the courtship lasted just long enough for him to get in the saddle and get her pointed in the right direction. Once the reins were snapped, the Mustang just indulged herself in doing what she'd been born to do.

That one thing, quite simply, was to run.

Clint kept his eye on the stagecoach when he could, but even that was a struggle. Between the wind gusting into his face and the dust that always seemed to fill every breath of desert air, Clint was having a hard enough time simply keeping his eyes open.

For the most part, he stuck to the open ground alongside the main trail. Clint gave himself enough distance so he could ride around the Marshals' wagon and even flank it without being spotted by a casual eye. There was always the chance that someone would see him, but that was just a risk he needed to take.

Steering Bobcat back toward the trail, Clint touched his heels to the Mustang's sides and then hung on for dear life. Before too long, he not only found the horse's rhythm, but he even started to relish the feeling of charging over the open land like a pure force of nature.

He kept the wagon's position in mind as he got himself toward a spot that should be well ahead of it. When he'd picked out that spot, Clint started pulling back on the reins. Bobcat didn't respond right away, but Clint hadn't expected her to.

Instead, Clint started treating the Mustang like a temperamental lady. He got her going in the right direction and gave her plenty of extra time and distance for her to throw her fits or exert her own will. By the time she was worn out from all of that, they were at the spot that Clint wanted to go in the first place.

As if picking up on what was going on, Bobcat started to fuss some more when Clint led her back in the direction of the trail.

"Too late now," Clint said. "We're already here."

He didn't think the horse would understand his words, but Bobcat seemed to comprehend the spirit behind them well enough. Either that, or she was more like a lady than even Clint would have guessed because now that she wasn't getting resistance, she no longer wanted to fight. Clint knew better than to think he'd actually tamed her and simply enjoyed the truce while it lasted.

The Mustang bolted across the trail and slowed to a trot once she reached the other side. From there, she responded to Clint's tugs upon the reins as though she'd suddenly become the most well mannered horse in the county.

Clint rode her a ways from the trail before turning her so she was facing roughly in the same direction as the wagon should have been headed. He waited there for a few moments, realizing that Bobcat had been moving even faster than he'd figured. After a bit more waiting than he'd originally anticipated, the rumble of wagon wheels could be heard.

Suddenly, he didn't like the idea of being away from the wagon for so long. Even though that was the plan, he would have much rather preferred to keep at least as close an eye as he did on the train. But that simply wasn't possible this time around and keeping some distance was the best insurance policy Clint could offer.

After all, if things were going to go wrong, being there in the middle of the mess wouldn't be as much help as being outside of it. At least on the outside, he could stay away from whatever storm was brewing and then choose the moment to throw himself into it. Of course, the trick was being able to have the instincts or the eyesight to know when that moment was.

As with most other gambles, it was one of those things that would ultimately make the difference. Sitting there, waiting for the coach to roll down the trail, Clint was getting a bad feeling in the pit of his stomach.

He didn't know what was causing it, but Clint had to trust that there was something more than just a bad bit of food at work. Something didn't feel right. Or maybe it didn't sound right. Before Clint could put his finger on it, the rumble of wagon wheels flooded his ears.

As the stagecoach drew closer, the trembling of the ground could be felt running up through the Mustang's body. Bobcat started to shift uncomfortably while throwing nervous glances toward the direction of the approaching wagon.

"It's all right, girl," Clint said soothingly. "I'm not about to let us get run over."

Lowering her head, Bobcat let out a huffing breath and kept still as the wagon thundered past them.

Clint turned to look toward the wagon but didn't want to strain his eyes while doing so. By the sound of it, that wagon was going as fast as that team could pull it and he wouldn't have more than a second to see as much as he could when it passed. He couldn't afford to waste that second.

He caught sight of the lead horses first. Their heads pumped furiously back and forth. The wild look in their eyes was unmistakable.

The next thing he saw was the front of the wagon as well as the two men in the driver's seat. One of them was hunched down low and gripping the reins in both hands. The other had his shotgun in front of him and was standing up while turning toward the wagon behind him.

As it rolled down the trail, Clint was able to see that the inside of the coach was bustling with activity as well. Most of the window was blocked by a man's torso. Even what Clint could see past that first man was only the front of another standing directly in front of him.

As far as he could tell, all of the men inside the coach were on their feet. The shotgunner was climbing back toward the coach and the driver was struggling to maintain control of his team. Clint may not have been inside that coach, but he didn't need to be to know that things weren't going too well there.

Before he could figure any of it out for certain, Clint's line of sight was washed away with bright earth tones as the stagecoach thundered down the trail and sped away. Now that it was no longer in his focus, the coach seemed to be flying away from him at a breakneck speed.

Clint's mind raced with possibilities.

He could take off after it right now and probably catch up to it within a minute. Knowing Bobcat, the Mustang would probably love another opportunity to break into a run. Then again, that might just tip his hand too soon. If there were men in danger inside the wagon, seeing Clint rush up to the side of the coach might be enough to light a very short fuse.

But if Clint forced himself to wait a few seconds and come up around the stagecoach on a blind side, he might be able to get the drop on whoever was causing trouble. He might just be able to get a notion of what the hell was going on in there as well.

It felt like a hand clenching around his gullet, but Clint gritted his teeth and bided just a little more time.

THIRTY-EIGHT

The tide of the fight had turned several times in as many seconds. One moment, it seemed as though Trask was going to have his day and wrest the gun out of Rivera's hands. The next moment, it seemed that Rivera was on the verge of taking Trask down for good. While Ike had his showdown with Redwater, this other fight seemed to be going on in a different part of town.

There were so many combinations of ways for things to end up and only a very few of them were good news for the lawmen.

Rather than worry about all the possibilities, every man inside that stage knew they had to see to their own survival first. One glance in the wrong direction would give their opponent just the opening they were looking for.

Not that Rivera had much of a chance to look in any other direction, however. It was all he could do to just keep his grip on his rifle. Trask still had ahold of his sleeve and refused to let go. It wasn't an overpowering grip by any means, but it did keep the Marshal from having his full range of movement. Every time Rivera tried to sneak in a good punch or pull away from the prisoner, he would come up short on that one side where Trask had ahold of him.

Trask bared his teeth in a vicious snarl. "You ain't getting away from this one, Marshal. I'll see us both dead before that happens."

The threat had been intended as a kind of verbal punch to throw Rivera off his balance. Rather than try to answer the threat or let himself be rattled by the venom in Trask's eyes, he knuckled down and gathered up all the energy he could into his captive arm.

From there, Rivera started pulling back as though he was desperately trying to get away. Trask grinned at the thought that he'd put the fear into Rivera to such a degree that the lawman wanted to get away from him. Since Rivera still had something he wanted, Trask wasn't about to let that happen.

Rivera kept tugging withz that one arm until he could feel Trask was pulling back with a good amount of strength. After getting the timing down just right, Rivera waited for Track to pull before snapping his arm forward at that same instant.

This time, Trask and Rivera were both moving in the same direction. The hitch was that the direction drew a short, straight line directly toward Trask's upper torso.

Rivera couldn't exactly be picky about where his punch landed, so he just had to make the best out of the one he got. Shifting his fist so he led his punch with his two biggest knuckles, the Marshal was able to twist his arm so that he managed to catch Trask at the base of his neck.

The prisoner's mouth dropped open and his eyes widened as he felt the Marshal's fist slam into his windpipe. It wasn't a solid blow, but there was enough behind it to stun him while also robbing him of his next couple of breaths. Reflexively, Trask's hands opened and he threw himself back against the wall.

Not missing a beat, Rivera gathered up his rifle and shifted around to see what was happening with the other men inside the stage. The scene he found was enough to take his own breath away. Kelso's front was covered in blood and Redwater's fist was drenched as well where still clenched around the handle of the knife.

Ike's eyes were intense slits and his hands were surprisingly steady upon his gun. "Think about this, Redwater," Ike said. "You're still alive now because nobody could hang a murder charge on you."

"Going to this new jail is just as good as death," Redwater answered in a low growl of a voice.

"That depends on how sure you are that you'll get out of here alive. You take this any further and you'll be catching lead for certain."

Redwater took a moment to let those words sink in. Even though Marshal Kelso was still squirming, the Indian hardly seemed to notice. His arms were like iron bands around the lawman: one around Kelso's neck and the other holding the blade firmly in place.

Now that both fights had come to a standstill for the moment, the rumbling of the wagon going over the trail was the only noise that filled the coach. That is, it was the only noise until the thumping of footsteps could be heard coming over the top of the wagon itself.

Trask was still sputtering for breath and trying to force out some garbled curses, but most of those weren't much more than strangled grunts. He shuffled back into a corner so he could get a look at what was going on without putting his back to any of it. Therefore, he was the first one to spot the figure looking down through the roof of the stage.

Like many models of its kind, the stage had a trapdoor on top of it to let in light as well as to let a bit of air flow through the inside. Standing on top of the stage and looking down over the barrel of his shotgun, the man who normally sat next to the driver took in the sight of what was going on.

"Put that man down!" the shotgunner said to Redwater.

The Indian knew better than to look up for himself. All

the other eyes in the stage were flicking up and down between him and the man atop the stage. Except for Kelso's. That one's eyes were starting to glaze over from pain and loss of blood.

"You heard me, red man!" the shotgunner yelled. His statement was punctuated by the double clicking of both of his weapon's hammers being pulled back. "Let him go."

"I let him go and he'll bleed out," Redwater stated simply.

The shotgunner seemed torn. He looked toward Ike and Rivera for guidance on what he should do next.

"So what, then?" Ike asked. "You got him and we don't want him to die. But if he's about to bleed out anyhow, then I don't see any reason why I shouldn't take you out with him."

Trask was still squirming against the wall. He was trying to suck in a breath, but kept coming up short. Although he was able to pull in some more air with every attempt, he was quickly approaching the panic of a drowning man. Every so often, he would look out a window and push his nose toward the frame so some more air could be forced into his lungs.

When he pulled his head back this time, most of the color had returned to his cheeks and his eyes were starting to clear up. Finally, he brought in a lungful of air and was able to keep it inside for a bit before blowing it out again. He took one more look out the window and then dropped back into his seat with the familiar smirk on his face.

"Might as well let him go," Trask said.

When Redwater turned to look at him, the motion was at a normal speed. Coming from him, however, it seemed to be an almost shocking display. In his eyes were equal parts question and challenge.

"You heard me," Trask said. "They might be able to sew up that Marshal if'n we get him to the closest town. That way, you won't have to hang for killing the prick."

The Indian relaxed a bit, but his grip remained solid as

rock. He looked around at the guns pointed in his direction and hardly seemed concerned by any of the barrels staring straight back at him. Instead, he seemed to be more fixated upon the eyes that were staring down those barrels.

"You sure about this?" Redwater asked.

"Yeah," Trask replied. He waited until Redwater was looking at him again before winking and adding, "Real sure."

Ike saw the wink as well. He didn't know exactly what it meant, but he knew it couldn't be good.

THIRTY-NINE

"All right," Trask said while leaning forward on his bench and bringing his hands up to wait height. "You got us. We took our shot and missed."

Without taking his eyes off of Redwater, Ike said, "Then ease back up against that wall and shut your mouth. Rivera, make sure he doesn't have some other surprise for us."

Although the Marshals weren't usually inclined to take an order from a guard, Rivera had no qualms about carrying out Ike's request. He shifted around so he was once again looking at Trask. This time, however, he had his gun firmly in hand.

Snapping his rifle forward, Rivera jammed the barrel into Trask's gut and used it to push him up against the wall. "Hold still," was all he said before using his free hand to pat Trask down.

On top of the stage, the shotgunner nervously shifted his aim from one prisoner to another. His legs shifted instinctively beneath him so he could keep his balance on top of the moving stage and his arms kept the shotgun amazingly steady.

"What's the word?" came a voice from the front of the stage.

"The driver wants to know if he should stop this wagon," the shotgunner explained.

"That depends on—" Ike's answer was cut short by the sound of gunfire crackling not too far away.

From this distance, and over the rumble of the wagon's wheels, the gunshots sounded like they were a good distance away. But none of the men were fooled by that. If they could hear the shots over all the ruckus around them, that meant the guns were real close.

The first shot or two came in quick succession. The next shot was hot on their heels and this time it was followed by the hiss of lead speeding through the air. The driver tightened his grip upon the reins and gave them a snap since the shots seemed to be coming from the side. On top of the stage, the shotgunner ducked down so quickly that he almost lost his balance and rolled off the edge.

Inside the stage, Redwater saw Ike's eyes shift away from them to look out at the source of the incoming gunfire. At that moment, the Indian ripped the knife from where it had been buried and flicked his wrist so that he was now holding it by the crimson-stained blade.

With a motion that was as quick as it was effortless, Redwater snapped his wrist again and sent the blade flying from between his fingers. The slippery blade seemed to give it a little extra spin as it turned once through the air, darted up toward the trap door and landed solidly in the shotgunner's throat.

The man on top of the stage looked stunned at first and then alarmed when he tried to take a breath. The air was blocked by the steel invading his neck and when he realized that, the pain flooded throughout his entire body.

His finger tensing on the trigger, the shotgunner tossed himself backward and onto the side of the roof. The shotgun roared and blasted out a chunk from the skylight's frame and the recoil took the weapon completely from his hands. He didn't notice either of those things, however, since he was too busy grabbing at the handle protruding from his throat.

He got a grip on the handle that was still warm from being clenched within Redwater's fist. With his vision starting to blur and his life flashing before his eyes, the shotgunner pulled at the knife to try and get the thing out of him. Not even when it was too late did he realize that the blade was curved at the end and sharper than most razors. Because of that curve, he opened his own throat even more as he tried pulling the knife out and flopped down dead on top of the stage after one last gasp.

All of this happened so fast that Ike was just turning to look back at Redwater before the shotgunner's body landed on the roof. Ike's face was now covered with blood that had been sent through the air by the Indian's blade. The shock of that turn of events was enough to put Ike off for a split second. That was all Redwater needed to make another move of his own.

When Ike was blinking away the blood that had splattered into his face, he found Redwater coming at him like a runaway bull. The Indian had both arms out and spread and he threw himself forward without even minding the chains that were still wrapped around the pole.

It was all Ike could do to brace himself before the Indian was landing on him like a boulder that had been dropped onto the stage from above. Ike twisted the rifle around to both keep the trigger away from Redwater's grasp while also using it to brace himself for the impact that was on its way.

Redwater landed heavily, but not as heavily as Ike was expecting. Most of the Indian's momentum was robbed from him when the chains snapped taut and kept him from following through on his charge.

Ike wasn't in a position to celebrate just yet, however, since one of Redwater's hands was still able to wrap around a part of the rifle.

"What the hell happened?" Ike asked while struggling with Redwater for control of the rifle.

Rivera still had Trask pinned against the wall and was doing a fairly good job of keeping his composure. "There's riders coming up on the stage from off the trail," the Spaniard said. "They're shooting at us."

Trask's breath came out in desperate gasps as it was pushed out of him by the rifle barrel in his stomach. "Damn right they're shooting at us," Trask snarled. "They're shooting at you is more like it."

Rivera was still in the process of patting Trask down and he finished that up before easing up in the least. As far as he could tell, Trask didn't have anything on him that didn't belong. Of course, that wasn't too big of a comfort at the moment.

"Ain't you even gonna tell us to give up before anyone else gets hurt?" Trask taunted.

Rivera set his jaw and said, "Too late for that."

The prisoner nodded. "Guess you're right. It's way too late for that."

FORTY

The riders had approached the trail from the left side of the stage. They'd come thundering in from the southwest like a storm, armed to the teeth and showing death in their eyes. Every one of the half dozen men wore double rig holsters and bandoliers to supply extra shells to the rifles in their hands. Even their horses seemed wild and untamed as they charged toward the stagecoach in a terrible wave.

As wild as they seemed, they still moved with a good amount of organization. They maintained their formation and even managed to keep relatively silent until the time came for them to make themselves known amid a shower of gunfire.

A signal from the lead rider brought all of the men's rifles to bear. Another signal had turned them toward the stagecoach's path and then gotten them flowing toward it with increased speed. They moved like a small army who were confident to have surprise working in their favor. The only thing they didn't know was that there was one person they hadn't surprised.

Clint had been tailing the band of riders for just under half an hour. While he would have liked to keep them in his sights for longer than that, he wouldn't have caught them at all if Bobcat hadn't gotten a wild hair and taken off on her own.

At the time, Clint had been real close to putting the spurs to the animal and whipping it harder than he ever liked to do. The Mustang went off seemingly on her own and threatened to put Clint's entire job and the lives of those Marshals at risk. But that tune changed when he'd gotten a look at where Bobcat was headed.

Perhaps the Mustang had caught a glimpse of the other riders or maybe had picked up on some kind of scent. Whichever it was really didn't matter since Clint got a look at them before too long. When he did, he not only changed his thoughts about the Mustang, but hunkered down and steered Bobcat more into the path she'd already chosen.

Clint noticed when the riders started heading in toward the trail and did his level best to cut them off before they got there. The hard fact was that they'd been preparing for this moment all too well and had allowed their horses to conserve their energy until the very moment it was needed. When the signal came, every one of those animals took off like their tails were on fire.

Not even Eclipse on his best day could have caught up to them any quicker than Bobcat did.

Clint rode low in the saddle and steered wide of the riders as Bobcat tore up the ground between them. Automatically, his hand reached down and drew the modified Colt. When Clint brought the gun up, his other hand was tugging the reins to bring the Mustang in for the first strike.

All of the riders wore bandannas over their faces to protect them against the swirling dust. As Clint approached the one at the back, the rider turned in his saddle and looked at him with wide, surprised eyes. He wasn't able to see the signal given by the riders' leader, since his plate was already more than full.

The remaining riders brought up their guns and Clint did the same. Instead of taking aim at the rider closest to him, he shifted the Colt toward the lead rider and squeezed off a shot. Although Clint wasn't able to take proper aim while compensating for the motion of the horse beneath him, one of the main reasons for the shot was to take away the element of surprise the riders were counting on.

Clint couldn't tell if he'd succeeded since he couldn't see how anyone on the stage was reacting. What he could see, on the other hand, was a whole bunch of pissed off riders turning in their saddles to get a look at him.

Reflexively, Clint pulled himself down low over Bobcat's neck as answering shots were thrown his way. Hot lead whipped through the air over his head. Taking a trick from a few Indian warriors he'd seen, Clint reached down beneath Bobcat's neck and fired off a shot from there rather than expose himself by sitting up straight.

Even though it was rushed, that shot managed to take a piece out of the rider at the head of the pack. The bullet drilled through his rib cage and crumpled the rider over just as he was about to take a shot at Clint. His body dropped halfway from the saddle, but he still managed to hold on before hitting the ground.

Clint pulled himself back up again and righted himself in his saddle as he and the rest of the riders kept moving headlong toward the stagecoach. Four of the riders peeled off from the group and headed for the stage, shooting at it as they went.

The remaining two hung back to deal with Clint. One of them was taking a shotgun from the holster on their saddle. The other was the one Clint had clipped with that last shot. Although blood was soaking into his jacket from the blackened wound, the fire in his eyes let it be known that he was anything but done.

Gunshots filled the air, as the horses tore across the sandy ground. Clint tried to keep an eye on the stage while also watching the riders coming straight for him. The one with the shotgun was his first concern since that double-barreled monster was already swinging around to look straight at him.

Touching his heels to Bobcat's sides, Clint pulled the reins hard in the direction of those riders and prayed that the Mustang still had plenty of steam left in her engine. It turned out that she not only responded well to Clint's direction, but thrived on it. Bobcat clamped down on her bit and pumped her legs furiously against the packed earth.

Before he could get to them, Clint saw the two riders that were meant for him turn in opposite directions and swing around to flank him on either side. He didn't even let them get comfortable where they were before Clint yanked the reins back and brought Bobcat to a halt.

The Mustang didn't respond well to that in the slightest, but Clint had been counting on that very thing. When the Mustang reared up and started pawing at the sky, Clint straightened up in the saddle, took quick aim and then fired off a round at the closest rider.

Less than a heartbeat away from pulling his own trigger, the rider felt the bullet drill through his chest. The impact was like getting kicked by an angry mule and sent him scrambling off the backside of his horse.

"One down," Clint thought. "Plenty more to go."

FORTY-ONE

As soon as Kelso's body dropped down far enough, Ike took a shot with his rifle. The gun's blast echoed within the coach and sent a ringing through everyone's ears that was almost deafening. Smoke billowed from the barrel to add a gritty, metallic taste to every breath.

But the target he'd been hoping to hit wasn't where it was the last time he'd seen it. Redwater had moved faster than a man his size had a right to and it didn't look as if he was going to stop anytime soon. The Indian had gotten onto the bench and was laying down as flat as his chains would allow.

Not even flinching as the rifle bullet whipped within inches of his head, Redwater leaned back and pulled his feet up until his knees touched his chest. From there, he placed both feet against the pole in front of him and inched his shoulders against the wall.

The stage was moving faster now and the voice of the driver could be heard yelling for the team to go even faster. The crack of leather snapped through the air and when the horses responded, the entire coach started rocking precariously back and forth.

When the wheels hit a hole in the road, the impact sent

everyone inside the wagon tumbling. It was all any of them could do to keep from winding up in a giant heap on the floor. All except for Redwater, of course. He had himself wedged in between the wall and the pole so well that he might have stayed there through an earthquake.

Although Ike managed to keep himself upright, the jostling caused his rifle to shake at the moment he was going to fire. His finger twitched on the trigger rather than giving it a smooth pull and the bullet punched a hole through the wall well over a foot from Redwater's head.

That was all the time the Indian had needed. Gritting his teeth, he summoned up as much strength as he could and for a man with his size and build, that was a hell of a lot. The muscles in his legs tensed into rock solid masses, shoving his feet forward and breaking the pole in front of him like a toothpick in the process.

The smile that came onto Redwater's face at that moment was the first time Ike had seen the Indian look like a normal, breathing person. It was also one of the most unnerving sights he'd ever seen in his life.

Redwater pulled his legs back and allowed the chains to come over the broken chunk of pole in the floor. All it took then was another snap of his wrists and his arms were free as well. Although the manacles were still locked around his wrists and ankles, Redwater was now free to move wherever he pleased. The first place he wanted to move was straight toward Ike.

The guard had been forced to duck to one side to avoid getting hit by the broken chunk of pole that came flying toward him. When he looked up, he was just in time to see the Indian coming at him like a nightmare. Both of Redwater's arms were outstretched and the chain hung between them.

Ike squeezed off a shot from the rifle, but it was more of a desperation play rather than anything he thought would do any damage. The shot not only missed Redwater, but it failed to even cause the Indian to flinch.

Redwater landed awkwardly, but managed to get his hands on the guard. That was all he'd wanted to do, and he gathered up the rest of his body after tightening his grip. One of his hands took hold of the barrel, causing the smell of burning flesh to fill the air. Redwater ignored the heat from the rifle and kept the barrel pointed away from him. He used his other hand to start looping the chain around Ike's neck.

Nearby, Rivera was losing the fight for his own weapon as well. Trask was still chained to the pole in front of him, but that didn't prevent him from lashing out with both feet to send kick after kick into any part of the Marshal he could reach. His boots landed on Rivera's shin, then his knee and a few times in his gut.

Every time a kick landed, Rivera tensed and prepared himself to shake it off. But the combined kicks were piling up and that was enough to loosen his grip on his gun.

Sensing his impending victory, Trask reached out to take hold of the rifle by its barrel and midsection. It was the only part of the weapon he could get his hands on and that was almost enough to allow him to claim the gun for himself.

Rivera felt the weapon being taken from him. First, it was wrenched from one hand and then it started wriggling free of the other. Trask had ahold of it and was shaking it like a hungry dog with a bone in its mouth. Moments before his fingers let the rifle go completely, Rivera managed to get a finger beneath the trigger guard.

Trask saw that immediately and knew it would take just one squeeze for a bullet to be sent right through the middle of his face. Since he knew he couldn't do anything about it that quickly, Trask did the next best thing and pushed the rifle straight back so the stock slammed into Rivera's face and the trigger was taken out of his reach.

The first thing Rivera felt was the sting of his finger getting jammed beneath the trigger guard. The next thing he felt was a hard, dull pain that knocked him back and made it feel as though the entire coach was rolling down a hill, end over end.

Still holding on to the rifle with one hand, Trask lunged forward to take advantage of an opportunity that was too good to pass up. While the Marshal was reeling from getting knocked in the face by the rifle butt, Trask found the ring of keys hanging from Rivera's belt and ripped them free. His mouth was practically watering as he tried the keys one at a time until he finally found one that fit into his manacles and turned perfectly within the locks.

"I've got a winner!" Trask announced gleefully.

In moments, he was free of all his restrains and the chains hit the floor noisily. He then turned his attention to Redwater, but the Indian was already on his way out. He was climbing up through the open trap door. Behind him, Ike was being dragged like a sack of potatoes, struggling and trying to free himself from the chain that was wrapped around his neck.

FORTY-TWO

Clint knew that every second that ticked by was more valuable than gold. Already, the remaining riders were converging on the stagecoach and giving the driver a run for his money. Clint knew there was a man riding shotgun as well, but there didn't seem to be any return fire of that caliber coming in the riders' direction.

That either meant that something had happened to the shotgunner or the man had frozen when he was needed most. Since the Marshals must have picked their men, Clint could only assume that the worst of those two had actually happened.

Snapping Bobcat's reins, Clint got the Mustang racing even faster to catch up to the stagecoach. But there was still one more rider close by he needed to contend with and that man wasn't about to be left behind. Pulling out his second pistol, the rider locked his eyes on Clint and brought the weapon around as his target drew closer.

Even though Clint had his Colt in hand, he decided against firing point blank at the man and instead got Bobcat to pour on just a little more speed. The Mustang charged forward and brought Clint to within arm's reach of the other rider. From there, Clint cocked his arm back and then swung the Colt forward until the handle of the pistol caught the man on the fresh wound in his side.

Doubling over in pain, the rider let out a yell and dropped the gun he'd been about to fire. He dropped his reins as well and within moments, he was the one that was dropping out of the saddle. His body crumpled in two and he hit the ground on his side.

Clint looked over his shoulder and saw the wounded man rolling in the dirt. Although the horse took off in another direction, the other man was still squirming on the ground until he was able to flop onto his back and try to sit up.

While Clint wouldn't have traded places with that one, at least he'd kept from having to kill another person. Clint took a note of where the man had landed and made a point to remember that he needed to go back there and check on him when this was done. Of course, there was always the tricky part of living that long.

Shifting back around in the saddle, Clint was surprised to find that Bobcat was still running like the wind and was even catching up to the stage as though that was her own personal mission. He didn't need to coax the Mustang any further, so Clint took a moment to reload his Colt while the horse did the rest.

When he got a little closer, Clint saw that his worst fear for the shotgunner had been confirmed. Although he couldn't see much more than shapes through the dust storm surrounding the moving stage, he did see that one of those shapes was a man's body laying on top of the stage itself. Since there was one figure in the driver's seat, that didn't leave many options as to the identity of the one on the roof.

The riders had fanned out and were doing a good job of surrounding the stagecoach. All the while, they fired their pistols up toward the driver and at the feet of the horses. Clint couldn't tell if they were trying to get the thing to stop or send it rolling into a boulder.

Rather than try to figure it out, Clint moved up as close

as he could get to them before the other riders noticed he was there.

The rider closest to him held out one arm and made some sort of signal. He must have assumed that Clint was one of the men that had been dispatched to help him, since it took another moment or two before he turned around to take a look at who was actually coming up alongside him.

When he saw that it was Clint, the rider immediately brought his guns around while twisting in the saddle to take aim. Before he could pull his trigger, Clint's modified Colt barked once and put a bullet through the man's skull.

The rider slumped back in the saddle and fell to one side. His feet caught in the stirrups and he dangled there for a while before he was finally knocked loose. His body hit the ground with a nasty thump and was crushed beneath the wheels of the wagon.

Clint could see the other three riders had positioned themselves around the stagecoach and were either reloading or taking better aim. Deciding that the most strategic place to be in any hurricane was the eye, Clint moved Bobcat a little closer and prepared himself for a leap of faith.

He'd seen the move performed by some trick riders, but Clint never fooled himself into thinking he was anywhere near as good as one of them. But, necessity was the ultimate inspiration, so he took his feet from the stirrups and swung one leg over Bobcat's back.

After getting his heel in one of the stirrups, Clint got his other heel positioned just in front of the saddle horn. Although he would have been a little more sure of himself if he'd had Eclipse's height for an added advantage, Clint knew that the Mustang was doing real well just keeping up to the stage with such relative ease.

Without taking a moment to think about what he was doing, Clint didn't give himself a chance to back out before pushing off the horse with both legs and reaching out to grab hold of the stage. His chest hit first and, for a terrifying moment, Clint thought for certain that he was going to slide right down to join the other rider as a bump in the road.

But before that could happen, Clint's hands found something to hold on to and his toes soon found purchase as well. He acted on sheer instinct as he climbed up the stage using grips that he didn't even see. At that moment, with the blood pounding through his veins, he might very well have kicked holes in the side of the stage with his own feet just to keep from falling off.

Before he knew how he'd made it, Clint found himself next to the driver. The man looked over at him with a stunned expression. Before he could get a word out, however, Clint pushed him down and drew his Colt in a fluid series of movements.

The pistol sent a bullet through the air that clipped one of the riders in the shoulder. It wasn't a lethal wound, but it was enough to send the rider spinning out of his saddle and onto the ground rushing by underfoot.

As Clint watched the rider bounce away, he saw the one who'd been in the lead easing his horse up to the side of the stage. The door swung open and Trask jumped out as though he thought he could fly. Thanks to some help from the rider, he made it onto the back of the horse and both of them peeled away.

Clint took quick aim and fired off a shot. Although the shot missed Trask, the rider directly in front of him winced as a little blood sprayed from his left shoulder. They kept riding away from the stage, however, and Clint knew they were as good as gone.

FORTY-THREE

Rivera felt helpless as he watched Ike get dragged up by his neck through the skylight. Somehow, Redwater had already crawled out onto the top of the stage, leaving Ike to dangle like a man from a noose. He'd already been unable to stop Trask from jumping out of the coach, but that was because Rivera had been too occupied by trying to figure a way to keep Ike alive.

The Marshal's first impulse was to take the keys Trask had left behind. But that would take too long to unlock the shackles. More than that, the chain he needed to unlock was around Redwater's wrists and those were well out of his reach.

So Rivera went for the next best thing and picked up one of the rifles laying on the floor. There were plenty to choose from since Ike's had slipped from his hands as well when he was yanked off his feet. Rivera got to the closest one, made sure there was a round in the chamber and took a breath to steady his aim.

He could see Ike's struggling was getting weaker by the second, so he didn't take too much time before pulling his trigger. The rifle bucked against his shoulder and filled the inside of the coach with thunder. Sparks exploded from the chain, sending a few metal fragments in every direction before Ike dropped back down inside with a heavy thump.

For a moment, the guard didn't seem to know what had happened. he reached up to feel the cuts in his face from the flying metal as well as the tender skin around his neck. The main thing was that he was alive and breathing and that was more than enough to make him smile with relief.

Up on top of the stage, Clint heard a rifle shot exploding from inside. That brought his attention toward the coach. The driver was looking back as well and before he could take a glance behind him, the end of a heavy chain swung through the air and caught him on the side of the head just above the ear.

The driver's eyes rolled back and he fell over, revealing the Indian crawling along the top of the coach like a giant insect. His eyes were firmly set upon Clint as his hand reached out to one side. Without even having to look toward the body laying on the roof, Redwater pulled the knife that had been lodged in the shotgunner's throat and reclaimed it for himself.

Clint jumped over the driver's seat so he could get to Redwater before the Indian put that knife to use again. Just as he was bringing his Colt around, he saw the Indian move like a gust of wind. He got his legs beneath him and lashed out with his knife to slice out toward Clint and down at a sharp angle.

A shot blasted up from inside the coach, but Redwater answered it by kicking the skylight shut with one foot. Even before the trapdoor dropped into place, the Indian was attacking Clint again. This time, he stood up and brought his knife up over his head to come lunging down again as Clint came forward.

Knowing he was only going to get one shot at this, Clint stopped himself short before colliding into Redwater and snapped both arms up as the Indian's were coming down.

He caught Redwater's knife arm in both hands, but could immediately feel that the Indian was too strong to be stopped that way.

Before Redwater lost his momentum, Clint twisted the man's wrist in another direction and then added his own strength to the mix. This time, it was Redwater who wanted to stop the knife, but it was too late for that. Clint had already gotten the blade redirected so that it hooked into a downward arc that brought it right into the Indian's gut.

Redwater staggered back and Clint let him go. The Indian's eyes grew wide as he looked down in disbelief at the knife protruding from his stomach.

Clint backed up a step so that he was standing in the driver's seat. He watched for a few more seconds, waiting for the Indian to drop. Instead, Redwater started sucking in breath and baring his teeth until he looked like a crazed animal.

Using the willpower he'd mustered, Redwater reached down and pulled the knife from his belly. Even as the blood flowed from his horrific wound, he charged forward while letting out a vicious war cry.

Clint dropped down to one knee, swept a hand down to the floor of the driver's seat and grabbed his Colt in the blink of an eye. When he brought it up and fired, he emptied the entire cylinder into the Indian's chest.

Redwater stumbled back and when he dropped onto the roof of the stage, the entire coach exploded beneath him. The rifle shots came up through the roof one after the other, making the Indian's body twitch and flop in a gruesome dance.

Finally, the thunder stopped and the trap door into the coach creaked open.

"Damn, Clint," Ike said. "I'm sure glad to see you."

"And I'm glad you knew it wasn't me who fell on that roof."

"Actually," Ike admitted, "that was more of a guess on my part."

Shaking his head while reloading the Colt, Clint looked around from his vantage point on the stage. "There's another rider around here."

"Don't worry about him," came Rivera's voice from inside the coach. "I picked him off while you two were dancing up there on the roof."

"Then that just leaves the one that got away," Clint said. "Where's Marshal Kelso?"

Ike's breath came out in a heavy gust. It seemed that all the strain from the entire ride had hit him at that very moment. "He's gone, Clint."

Still not quite thinking clearly, Clint asked, "Where is he?"

The moment he saw the look on Ike's face, Clint was sobered up from the rush that had taken him over during the fight. He knew what had happened even before Ike said another word. Looking inside the bloodstained coach filled in the rest of the gaps.

"Where's the closest town?" Clint asked.

"A place called Silver Strike isn't more than a few miles away," Ike said.

"Then that's where we're headed."

FORTY-FOUR

Silver Strike was a boomtown in every sense of the word. It was small and looked as though it had been put together so quickly that most of it would buckle under if a stiff wind came by. Like most other boomtowns, Silver Strike was made up of more saloons and brothels than shops or houses. It was the dead of night by the time Clint and Ike came riding down the main street and not one person seemed to notice the two newest arrivals.

"You sure you don't want me to come with you?" Ike asked.

Clint didn't even make eye contact. He was too busy looking over the other faces around him. "I'm sure. Just stay close and keep your eyes open."

"And you're sure Trask'll be around here?"

"We couldn't find much, but the trail I did pick up headed this way. I figured he'd head to the closest town to hole up and that clenched it. Hiding out somewhere like this would be a whole lot easier than camping. Besides, Trask needs some supplies and will be after some comforts. He's been in prison a long time, after all."

Ike nodded. "You got a point there. What if he ain't here?"

176

"Then we'll move on and keep looking. After all I've been through, I'm not about to let up until this job is over." He paused as a grim look came over him. "I owe Marshal Kelso that much at least."

Thinking about the way Kelso had died, pale and shriveled after bleeding out in that stage, Ike took on a grim look as well. "I'll be with you for as long as it takes. Kelso was a good man."

"Then find someplace to lay low and keep your eyes and ears open. If we play our cards right, we won't have to look much further than this very town."

"What am I waiting for?"

"I don't know, but you'll know it when it comes."

With that, Ike lowered his head so his face was mostly covered by his hat and steered his horse down another smaller street. Clint kept riding straight toward the source of the most commotion. He didn't even have to look to know that would be the town's entertainment district. Before he got in sight of all the drunks, gamblers and working girls, Clint forced a more sociable expression onto his face and slowed Bobcat to an easy gait.

Soon, Clint spotted a familiar face. It wasn't exactly the one he'd been expecting, however, and he was unable to keep that from showing on his face.

As for Heather, however, she looked like she was just out for another nightly walk.

"Clint! Fancy meeting you here!"

Clint gave her a wave and tipped his hat. "You're a sight for sore eyes."

"I thought you had some business in Tombstone."

"Business is over," he said.

Reaching up to take Clint's hand, Heather all but pulled him down from his saddle. "Well then. That must mean it's time for some pleasure."

• • •

Heather didn't want to wait for Clint to get her clothes off.
The moment they were in her room, she was tugging at his
belt and kissing him hungrily anywhere she could. Clint
responded in kind, moving his hands over her body as
though he couldn't wait to get more of her.

Just when she was about to take Clint's gun belt off, she
felt his hands clamp down around her wrists. She looked
up at him and found herself becoming more excited the
tighter he held on to her.

"Turn around," he whispered.

She did as she was told, putting her back to him while
bending at the waist so she could place her hands on a chair
next to her bed. Clint's hands slid over her waist and then
traveled down her legs.

"Don't forget to take your gun off," she purred. "Wouldn't
want anyone getting hurt."

"It's already off," he said. "And speaking of things that
need to be off . . ." Clint let that trail off as he pulled up her
skirts and started tugging at her frilly panties.

"So what brings you here?" he asked as his hand slid up
between her thighs.

"I'm meeting—"

She pulled in a quick breath as Clint's fingers found a
sensitive spot between her legs.

"Meeting who?"

"Oh, just a friend."

"Is that the same friend that gave you that bandanna
over there?"

Heather's eyes snapped open and locked upon the bandanna that was sticking out of one of her bags in the corner.
When she tried to turn around, Clint's hands tightened
around her waist, keeping her in front of him with her back
turned.

His hands moved up her back until one of them touched
her shoulder. With a tug just strong enough to pull down

the sleeve of her dress, he revealed a fresh wound covered by a few layers of bandages. "I would ask about this wound, but I already know who gave that to you."

Pulling away from him, Heather ran for her bags. She was stopped by Clint's hand locking around her dress and halting her just short of the gun hidden beneath her bandanna. She might have made another reach for the gun, but froze when she looked to see that Clint's gun belt was still around his waist and his hand was close to the Colt's grip.

"I was hoping to find someone from the train," Clint said. "It only makes sense that whoever planted the weapons in that toilet would be the same ones to arrange for a pickup along the stagecoach's route. I didn't expect it to be you. Then again, seeing as how well you distracted me, I guess that only makes sense."

Heather's face shifted back to her seductive smile. "It started out that way, but the time we had . . . that was something else entirely."

"Cut the sweet talk," Clint said. "Where is he?"

"Where is who?"

"You know damn well who. Where's Trask?"

Clint had learned more life-saving tricks sitting around a poker table than most men did from an Army instructor. That was how he knew to keep a real close eye on Heather the moment he asked her that question. There was a split-second where someone's reflexes answered even as their mouth and brain tried to hold out.

Heather's reflexes were to look toward the closet next to the bed. When Clint heard something move in that area, he reacted on his own instincts.

The door was kicked from the inside, but only swung open halfway before Clint's Colt was drawn and a shot was fired. Trask crouched in the darkness with a gun in hand and a wide-eyed expression on his face.

Clint's bullet had clipped the lobe from the prisoner's left ear and subsequently drained every bit of color from his face.

Slowly, Trask let the gun slip from his fingers as a smirk crept onto his face. "Y . . . you missed."

"You think so?" Clint replied.

FORTY-FIVE

"You bastard! You son of a bitch! You goddamn son of a bitch!"

Trask screamed every profanity he could think of at Clint as well as a few nobody had even heard of. He did so at the top of his lungs and from behind a new set of thick iron bars.

"You did it," Ike said. He stood next to Clint and Rivera, looking in on Trask as if the man was on exhibit inside a zoo. "You managed to haul his ass all the way out here."

"Well, after all I heard about this place, I had to see it for myself." Clint looked around at where he was. As promised by the Marshals, the prison was several day's ride from nowhere in a spot that made Trask's last prison seem like a garden in comparison.

"What do you think?" Ike asked.

"It's hell on earth."

Rivera nodded. "It probably won't be too long before that bitch you found in Silver Strike joins him here. After what she pulled, she'll either wind up here or hanging from a noose."

"My money's on this place," Ike said. "If Trask or Redwater didn't get a noose, she should be able to get out of it."

181

"Redwater got what he had coming," Rivera said. "Thanks to you, Clint."

"I wish I could have done more."

Ike shook his head as Trask kept right on spitting curses at all three of them. "I still say you should have shot this asshole when he came at you. You'd have been completely justified."

"Sure," Clint agreed. "But that wouldn't be justice. Trask and Heather loved running wild and doing what they pleased. They lived to raise hell and go wherever they wanted. Now, those days are over. He's had his last ride and out here, nobody will even remember that he was ever on this earth."

Both Ike and Rivera smiled at that and turned to look at Trask. Already, the prisoner looked panicked and desperate.

"I guess he still didn't kill anyone," Ike said with a shrug.

Rivera started laughing. "You know something? I'll bet Kelso would have gotten a kick out of this."

"Yeah," Clint said. "I like to think he would."

Watch for

RIDING THE WHIRLWIND

283rd novel in the exciting GUNSMITH series
from Jove

Coming in July!

J. R. ROBERTS

THE GUNSMITH

GIANT ACTION! GIANT ADVENTURE!

THE GUNSMITH

GIANT

GIANT WESTERNS FEATURING THE GUNSMITH

THE GHOST OF BILLY THE KID
0-515-13622-0

LITTLE SURESHOT AND THE WILD WEST SHOW
0-515-13851-7

J799

LONGARM

Explore the exciting Old West with one
of the men who made it wild!